Make The Road By Walking

by

Todd Lazarski

red giant books

For Bryan

"Beware, O wanderer, the road is walking too."
-Rainer Maria Rilke

Intro

Being laid-off is a bit like a drive to the airport when you're afraid, at least a bit, of flying. Every aspect of life begins that indefinable cataloging process: shit taken care of, scars earned, mountains climbed, lessons learned, jokes cracked, jump shots made, women laid, beers tried, communal hearty laughing moments of camaraderie that would slide easily into a Woody Allen end-of-movie montage, a la Annie Hall... And then there's the barreling tumult of everything else. All that meant to do, all that promise, all those empty pages, unlearned songs, unseen cities, all my moments of supreme, pummeling selfish dickheadedness, all those non-contributions now, tragically and certainly, gone down an endless drain, PVC-slick probably, because I'm leaving, and without doubt, never coming back.

Simple, stupid: Everything looks *that* much more important. Every passing building out the window attaining some new poetic hue through the filter of rain and the cab's back window, each face in an adjacent car a lifelong friend never met. The *'member when*s always run in melancholic slide-show behind my eyes, while Elliot Smith, or some such business, plays gentle, maudlin chords in my ears. Always, as if this journey about to be taken is on par with Magellan, Kerouac, that crazy French bastard traversing the Twin Towers on a shoelace, Lloyd and Harry on the moped. This is a dangerous, risky, pit-fall laden sojourn. No matter the what or the where. One two-hour flight? *Well, excuuuse me, Mr. Senor Ponce de*

Leon. An overly-romantic skew, just maybe, but with such mindset few things are nobler than getting into the back of a cab, sighing, and exhaustedly, bravely, requesting in the breathe of a man with a great weight pushing on his sturdy shoulders, "Airport"…

As if this didn't take place all around you, every day, on an unthinkable scale. As if there weren't 4,000 domestic fucking flights in the air at this very moment.

But numbers deceive, muddle, water down sentiments and hugeness. And what is wounding news if not an excuse, a great impenetrable permission granted to wallow in self-importance?

It takes a short-sighted man not to seize such opportunity. Or some kind of pragmatist, or, maybe, realist. Few things are worse: the kind not attuned to the prospects that just blew in with a mean winter storm (*maybe you'll get a snow day!*). One with concerns of the dollar and the rent and bills and those things and adult-ish constricting terms that come in my mother's laundry-list litany, just prior to 'stability' and right after 'responsibility.' Of the gauntlet of motherly spiels, none are harder to stomach.

Especially, now, suddenly with co-workers – ex-co-workers, or when does the 'ex' enter the term? – looking at you with that face, when they are buying you endless drinks at the normal Friday happy-hour watering hole on a Tuesday, taking you out for last lunches to "wherever you wanna go" (*half a work-week's worth of Philly cheesesteaks would indeed send me nicely on my way, thank you*), the boss even showing something approaching – what is that? what's his deal? Constipation? Newly dead mother he wants to open up about? It taking a head-scratching moment to sink in - *acknowledgement*. Ah, yesss. There it is. Respect? No bubs, you're on your way out.

But, if you know how, can smell the unpleasantness brewing and turn your collar up in the right fashion, few things are better than the chance to play the brave, unaffected martyr. I found myself those first few days, head held high, hands cupping a mug of steaming coffee, like in a funeral home, the victim, but the strong one, the survivor, the one Jodie Foster might play with bags under glassy eyes, weak smiles but trying, thinking of her children or that aging father that still needs care and strength, uttering the lines "it'll be for the best," "this is an opportunity," the term "explore" was sprinkled about the office with some of it's synonyms, and my go-to: "I'm not too worried." Offered, almost heroically, while waiting for any opening to slip in a subtle request for another pity burrito.

And as steeped in shit, slogans, empty optimism and smirking self-love as it all was, ignorance, maybe, and a weird kind of palm-sweating excitement impeded any true sense of concern. "I'm not too worried," I found myself uttering for about the 17th time two days later. And I wasn't. Told I was expendable, told 'this is real tough', told, 'but, ya know, times are hard,' told about the 'numbers,' told about my 'great assests', told about the 'economy', told about how 'sorry' they were, told about my 'severance' (*ay-oh!*), the world suddenly seemed to revert back to my 18-year-old daze. Where I was *owed* something. Where the pearl, everything, somewhere, would be handed to me. Like a college-bound jackass, infatuated with his own newfangled possibility. After all: ninety percent of all the blues and rock ingested on a daily basis was about just *this* – hitting the road with little regard to how, or if, one might make it home. Hank Williams had made a rock star career out of the sentiment and 3 open chords. Dreams: To experience the rush of wind through the cracked door of a westbound freighter, to throw back the warm covers of the sleep of mild men, to live a life of aimful, dusty-booted wandering. To exercise simple, bold loafing. To write, all hours of the night now, no concern for the clock, and with all that guitar business, too, yes, carry on with that, yes, mmmhhhm. Oh the chords I might find. To - as all those fortunate enough to have imbibed from-the-source Guinness and Chianti on the parents' dime for a semester always referred to it as – "find myself."

The words that might flow, tumble, cascade, one day, like so many bosoms out of too-tight tank tops. Where they sit there, unnaturally enslaved, by society, itching for the O2, freedom, *presentation*, clarity of thought. I can see myself scribbling with a cappuccino at a cafe in an unnamed, vaguely European town. Half-rumpled Seersucker suit and Dylanesque shades, a writerly beard. The slouching waiters know me, can't stand me in their gruff, ethnic way. Talk shit in their native tongue: *puta, nuttesohn*, whatever it is in French, maybe. But they tolerate me, the man. Respect enters in when they glimpse my inherent understanding of local custom, my endless dedication to a vision, to my loner-dom, to this boozy craft.

Little fear entered the equation as far as any of the former co-workers could see. They'd startle me from behind, on last smoke breaks of those last days, catch me staring poetically out over the parking lot from the loading dock smoke station. Picture me picturing Tanzania, or some such business, lost on a Proustian flight of my literary revelry. To them something too high-brow to comprehend – though of course I'm never condescending, always patient, curious with their curiosity. See me, profile enshrouded in Camel puff, head tilted slightly skyward, always a hint of rain on the horizon and a dusty mass market by someone you've never heard of stuffed into my jacket pocket. Wonder to where I was bound. Shake their heads at the misfortune, at my stoic bravery. Or, how I picture it, anyways – pity-savorer, I am. Slurp, slurp, and another round, sure.

What courage.

What spirit.

Let's take him out, this, the greatest shipper/receiver I've seen in all my two-and-a-half years here, and get 'em good and piss drunk.

Like I had joined the army. Oh, there would be tearful goodbyes, the what-will-you-do, concerned-eyes probing, the Teddy-if-you-ever-get-lonely-over-there-take-this-picture-and-think-of-me from that girl in Sales, arms around my shoulders, me being *the* excuse made on cell phones to wives to stay out late, Jameson shots all around, Pale Ales by the baleful. And me, lapping it all up. The brews, for sure. But the vibes – good-willed, sympathetic, a tad guilty ("oh, you *didn't* get laid off?") – more than anything. On night number four of this, with my personal possessions box under my arm, it's presence exclamation-pointing the *Leaving*, then later, me forgetting all about it and *leaving* it on a bar stool – it really only full of crinkled old quarter-read New Yorkers and a tennis ball that I occasionally flexed when the boss was around to feign stress – I'm as drunk as a nascent sailor, bleary-eyed and ready, leaning toward adventure and new lands and the romance of existing only in memories in this Podunk shit town straight out of a Springsteen tune. Enjoying the blissful, birthday-esque negligence of even for a second thinking about paying for a drink ("Scotch!"). Or the cab ("Fuuuck the bus"). Or the pizza delivery guy once I stumble back into my apartment, well after bar time. And the Roommate, who by now is a bit concerned for his own future interests, but sympathetic, sets down the remote, taps his ass-pocket and pulls out a twenty... "So it begins," I tell him, taking his money, a twisted smirk across my dumb ruby cheeks as I kick off my work boots, stumble over the rug, and make my way to the door to collect my pie and leave the driver with, certainly, his biggest tip of this Wednesday night. Later, going to bed, without thinking, by society-chiseled instinct I set the alarm, turn over, pick up a book – some minor Kerouac about loafing, dreaming – scratch my head, furrow my brow at the fuzzy endless kind-of rhythmic lines, scratch my balls, turn back over, and flip the alarm switch to 'off'...

Like that, suddenly and head-achingly, it is the next day. 2:33. PM... The sun shining through the blinds the same as any day, the sound of cars on the street similar if not just a bit more spaced-out, sporadic for the afternoon hour. Dead-spider splotches the same brownish hue on my plaster ceiling as they were when employed. Stagnant glass of hangover-water on the nightstand, by now growing bubbles on the surface. Cats, in the hall, and I can sense some wonder in their eyes as to my mid-day presence in their lives, but a simple sniff of my feet, and they continue on with the day.

Nowhere to be and nothing to do, my ill-conceived psuedo-vacation starts on a surprisingly melancholic tone: No missed calls on the cell, no stern voicemails, no wondering as to my whereabouts, no schedules interrupted by absence, no reported failures in operation, no attendance issues. For the first time since college I have slept away the morning and beginning of the afternoon, and awoken quite certain that not one utterance around the city is resembling, "where the fuck is Rawski?"

As far as I can tell, not one thing has gone awry from my temporary bed-residency.

Thing is: this is the retreat from the *everyday* that is nearly definitive of my most reoccurring fantasies. The no-alarm clock, no-shower, no-morning existence. Straight to the afternoon, no appetizer needed, thank you. Once-described as having two speeds – slow, and stop – if ever I were to thrive, this is the manner in which it would be done. In grade school, when asked to pen an essay describing 'What You Can't Wait To Do', I strayed from all those classmates that yearned to drive, buy a house, have a family – I couldn't wait to *Retire*. Not to mention my weird fascination, yes, call it envy, for anyone I see on TV hindered, blessed with the sexiest of afflictions – 'bedridden.'

Yet, a gnawing sense that something is amiss, that my long daydreamed Desert Island isn't, in fact, on the ocean. The feeling began to creep in, then, a sound in my mind that I would soon become all too familiar with, something like traffic from a distance, something like the hint of voices on the other side of the bathroom door when

I've sequestered myself, on the toilet, with a book, the exhaust fan turned up high: that of the world going on without me.

And thus, obviously, quickly, with all heart, with marbles out – the pen to the paper. The search, this time amplified and provided a solid sense of urgency. No mere 10-cents-a-word pittances for awkward polemics in my city's weekly rag. No more once-in-a-while stabs at musical 'criticism.' No more minimum requirements to render myself eligible for the preferred, long-sought, at-a-bar phrase, 'I'm trying to be a writer.' My side gig – fulfilling no doubt – is suddenly insufficient in light of recent developments. Something – *Something* – has to be done in response to this new pet, this heel-nipping, dim-witted, sharp-toothed animal, this relentless threat of tumbling inconsequence. Something of substance, something of magnanimity, something of girth and grit.

So the righteousness ebbs and flows. Certainly. But enough time over those first couple weeks spent pondering as to how much unemployment might come out to, enough glassy-eyed takes of late-night Stevan Seagal flicks, enough chronic ignorance as to the day of the week, and it was nigh impossible not to search for something. For something else.

Of course, always picturing myself one of those writers with that perfect, esoteric quote to start a piece of work, that seemed a likely impetus. A good one says so much about the author: I'm well-read, philosophical, have a point to this pontificating, can remember, you know, *stuff*. And the sudden lack of anything to do during the day allowed the stumble-upon of just such a passage (Who has time for Faulkner while gainfully-employed?):

"I notice how it takes a lazy man, a man that hates moving, to get set on moving once he does get started off, the same as he was set on staying still, like it ain't the moving he hates so much as the starting and the stopping. And like he would be kind of proud of whatever come up to make the moving or the setting still look hard.

He set there on the wagon, hunched up, blinking, listening to us tell about how quick the bridge went and how high the water was, and I be durn if he didn't act like he was proud of it, like he had made the river rise himself."

I be durn, indeed.

The lazy man being myself, perhaps this is merely a woe-begotten proclamation to defy the odds stacked in the world's corner. To point out a man's misfortunes and bask gloriously in them as I milk another round of drinks.

But progress is fleeting and rarely achieved from bed. So, when everything hit the proverbial fan and splattered steaming diahrrea over the white walls of what passed for a moderately acceptable early-20-something stab at adulthood, there began an effort to get and stay moving, to keep the laziness, mostly, purposeful. And a stride came to make the road by walking. In more or less a hope that I'll continue to get into that cab, have a reason to be so exhausted, so utterly tried when I direct the driver, coolly, evenly, turning my collar up, "airport, please."

1

There are really only two kinds of people in the world: those who encounter a state of sudden, imminent joblessness with the likes of teary phone calls, resume updates, Careerbuilder searches, newfound anger toward a once-appreciated employer, self-pity, Monster searches, spite, self-loathing, anxiety, Craigslist searches, or other general angsty bouts of 'what am *I* going to do!?' sentiment – most carried out with arms clasped over the back of the head and accompanied by long, breezy, drawn-out sighs…

And there are those who plan a vacation.

Yes, in actuality, vacation is not really the word at all for a post-layoff journey. The unemployed don't take vacations just like the homeless don't.

Where you going?

Vacation.

Motherfucker you're walkin' to the corner for cigs!

Proper handle or not, the time for solo walking is undoubtedly at foot. External forces – vindictive, heartless – have put me solely on the outsider's path. Now, smirkingly, I may never be back: the road, pointing west, always pointing west, stretches on for days in my mind, cardboard signs with far-flung destinations scribbled in Sharpie are in hand as I stand by the side of the highway, a tattered rucksack flung over the shoulder, guitar on back, a scruffy dog, inexplicably, by my side. Hitching, but only when there isn't a freighter close by. Cans of beans for supper and a highway overpass to nightly cover my head. I can hear a harmonica wailing by tin drum firelight in the background, see the bands of noble outsiders who might share my trail, however briefly.

What do they call you?

They call me the Milwaukee Kid.

Ain't got no home?

Ain't got no home.

And then I will be on my way. Hoisting the sack (maybe tied to the end of a stick? Shit, what kind of knot is that?) and turning with the brief adieu's of strong-willed men, too wise and seasoned to linger on drawn out goodbyes. Too hard. There will be days without bread and nights without roof. Tattered boots will be my plot. Sanctuary, only of the mind, mattresses and hot showers merely of the memory. But how I will come to embrace the stink. The stink! The putrid sweat running, down my legs, through the pubes, over yesterday's salt, causing stained long johns to stick to the body hair, rip it out in spots. My former cohorts fresh, stiff and shampooed and perfumed at their desks, pitying and wondering over me, forgetting me by degrees; while I give remorse for their simple day-to-day lives – dominated by the calendar, contained within the universe of desk chair and incessant bright computer screen – as I stand on the top of a mountain. The wind and the ocean blowing through my thick, hard-won beard. Yes, a mountain. Which mountain? Tough to say. Not only have I no interest in mountains or climbing or heights or pushing myself to the limit or such, but I have almost no concept of geology or geography, and aside from the fact that I was in the Adirondacks once as a kid, couldn't come close to naming a single domestic peak. But how I picture it. Maybe even sticking a flag of some sort into the ground, or flinging something – someone's ashes? – symbolically, stoically from the lofty heights. My dreams, with bits borrowed from a 'Rocky' montage, flashing before my very eyes.

Guiding my Internet to Orbitz one lonely afternoon, pensively sipping coffee in my sweats, while the world furrows its brows and uselessly pushes papers around oak desks, I feel thankful, and something remembered a-tugging.

It was really not too long ago: drinking expensive beer on a cheap couch, with no concept of rent, high on good pot and with endless 2am cigarettes dangling poetically from my mouth, a mouth that was spewing "ya know man's," earnestly, heartfelt, "I'm not goin' do it," "I'm not gonna play the game." John Lennon was probably playing at this point. "Working Class Hero" or some such business. As me and the like-minded soul, whom I shared the dust-bunny ridden edge-of-campus apartment with, were metaphorically arms-around-shoulders-ing each other. "Yeah," our heads nodding vigorously now, like Beats, or like how we pictured the Beats, in unison, in our flannel shirts, in black-and-white in our minds, smoke wafts all around us, his girl waiting patiently to hand the pipe back to me. Waiting for me to finish my rap: "What the fuck is a *career* anyway?"

How the italics would careen through those late night sentences. How I'd use my index finger. How *strong* we were, and the world, *Weak!*

Only to let it all lapse, into a two-year hamster-wheel cycle of schlepping boxes of books onto scales, paperwork, making with the nice in the inter-office politics, worrying about the rent. Becoming placated. Content. Worthless. Stuck. A sucker, born in stages. Breaking down like inflicted by M.S. Said couch seeming like the biggest deal. Hell – maybe I should even buy a new couch. Domestication working toward the brain like a syphilitic worm.

Maybe for the first time – remembering those silly but inspired spring nights of senior year, with graduation bearing down like a freight train of reality, with the warm evenings feeling endless and hinting oppressive at once, the fervent wish to cling onto something childish, even as it slips through our fingers, the soulful late night howlings of "I just wanna write, Man!" – did everything seem evident. Clear.

Such a subtle change in consciousness! There you are, Teddy - the nuts and bolts of weighty, serious, high-minded works of literature. The canon. Remember? 600 pages-plus. Easy. I can ring that out before the severance dries up.

And there is that whole issue. Severance. Limbs lost, cut away in bloody hacks. The attempted band aide toward acrimony, rupture, spurting arteries. An autopsy on what was just-getting-by. A reckoning of all you're leaving behind, which was so little. And you weren't given a choice, either.

Such an ugly, ruthless, yes, *severe*, word. Such a fantastic notion.

How is he to maintain living, eating? We took his livelihood; let's at least not kill the poor bastard.

Agreed. We will pay him full salary for 2 months.

To do nothing?

To do nothing.

So perhaps the forthcoming route is somewhat less penniless, hardscrabble than that of Jack London. Maybe there will be a debit card, with cell phone to check funds, maybe there will be direct deposit. There surely will be no tent, hostels or 1-star rooms. And of course the itinerary, not yet even committed to ink, is already pre-littered with the daily obligation, promised, sworn to, of checking in with the big mama (Kerouac did it too, ok?). Regardless: the gentle rolls of my beloved San Francisco call my name.

And I think of my heroes, them staring spine-first from the dusty bookshelf. All of them, and how, suddenly, thrust-about so, I've never been closer. Thrown to the point of fully realized, vindictive, and defiant self-smirking. To the point of 'goin out west where they 'ppreciate me'. And I'm hitting 'Book It,' with the worries of money, and explaining to my mother why I was taking a trip to celebrate dismissal from the graces of gainful society, washing away. Insolently, wondrously, I now begin the interior running song of the soul, someone's soul: *I'm gonna do what I want and I'm gonna get paid*. In a poignant scowl, with hat low over the eyes, jacket torn a bit, my heart beating like the train I'd soon come to ride, getting up to pour an afternoon drink, pumping my fist.

2

Uncle John never answered the phone. Wouldn't hear of it. Flat would not hear it. Not during basketball season – nor baseball or football for that matter – but especially not during hoops season, with the shoe squeaks and sweat and bright wood-colored high def background a source of strength, nightly continuity, a moving glowing pleasure in the winter months that for me signified Milwaukee winter and subsequent pain, but for John meant something else, colder, maybe. Especially during these now-nascent stages of March Madness. "I was watching the game," he would say, inevitably, always, whether Warriors, Raiders, A's or Bears depended only on the calendar, and box score analysis and capricious color commentary would impulsively preface his call back well before a pleasantry, a 'how's it going?' or, now, interest in my career status.

Phone ringing…

"See what fucking Jackson did Tuesday night?"

"Don't even get me started on fucking Jackson!"

Like that I was ready, for the rhythm, to hit the ground running, where others might hold hands in air and step back; my love for the intricacies of playoff races, fundamental soundness and shooting percentage both door and welcome mat into the realm of my father's only brother. The world of California's golden coast, that mystique and beckoning fog, all somehow shored up in the performance and latest statistics of whichever team out there had most recently taken the field. Or court. Or, even – in my sluttier moments of sports fandom - the ice.

With so much a-swirl in the forebrain of standard operating decision though, it all spinning through my muddled bean like the

14

last time I had seen Seagal (last night) in one of those late-night cable TV roundhouse kicks, rather than discuss Sweet 16 picks and *then* explain the joblessness, I decide to send a warning email and begin hedging bets on degrees of welcom-ness in Northern California. Hitting 'Send,' the subject line reading 'Get ready...', I see it as a first in a series, hopefully, of actions geared to let the chips fall where they may. This is how Neal would do it, I tell myself, actually uttering it aloud, framing Old Moriarty in my head for the third or fourth time today. Picturing greasy hair and stubble, a man with a cigarette pack rolled in his shirtsleeves, arm outstretched, thumb free and erect at the end of a veiny hairy arm, unconcerned, shoulders shrugging – *ya don't wanna stop, ya don't wanna stop* – but yearning his way west, all nonchalance and frequently stopping for a smoke, always lit with a match, or maybe a zippo, popping a squat roadside, butt in the dirt and elbows on knees, it always almost about to rain, background always lit in gray, wide Leone-esque vistas of *the* American West, eyes in speeding backseats a-wonder, questions posed to parents and significant others, as to the nature of the man.

Whaddya think's wrong with him?

Should we pick him up?

Looks insane to me.

Handsome though, in that ugly kind of way.

Does he know he's standing on the wrong side of the road?

Sure, email diminishes some of that black-and-white authenticity. And, yes, Neal's flight would have been sans thought of airplane, or Orbitz. *How would he even plan it then?* Regardless, a deviation. A flickoff of modus operandi. I don't even care what day of the week I leave, flashing on Peter Fonda discarding his watch in that early scene of Easy Rider. I could take a goddamn plane on a goddamn Monday.

As soon as the airline itinerary info enters the limbo of the Internet – the trip suddenly consummated, conceived with the 'Submit' button, me, at once becoming pro-life about the whole thing – bags are located at the back of the closet and the wheels set in furious, irreversible motion. My palms flare up, greasify like the skillet I've come to daily depend upon. Crispy afternoon bacon and coffee being the one thing to get me out of the darkness, away from the blanket, the ultimate of comforts if I have to, must be erect for a bit.

But at least I don't have to get dressed, fuckers!

Who are you talking to?

The cats wonder, go back to their walk around-and-sniff, nine-to-nine business.

Flannel shirts are de-hangered and laid half-neatly on the bed, a dog-eared copy of "Desolation Angels" is index fingered-down from a dusty bookshelf, flipped through, gotten misty-eyed over. I locate a long-forgotten umbrella, picture myself holding it, throw it again to the rear annals of the closet. Nearly every single sock in my dresser is pulled, brought to the basement laundry room, hopes are laid that some might come out magically in pair form. I begin to peruse the kitchen cupboards for a can of beans.

It is there, caught by the bottom corner of my eye, alongside the Shrimp Truck reminder postcard and an Urban Outfitters spring catalog (not anytime soon, my faux boho friends!). My mail. The ambitious Roommate – one who insisted on setting his alarm clock every morning, then letting it ring obtrusively, then banging around our apartment with the gall and faucet-turning-on clout that people with places to be sometimes have, and who upon finding me on the couch after each day of the past week, undressed, remote in hand, thought it quite hilarious to inquire, "How's retirement?" – had laid the stamped present for me on top of the pile, next to the Mr. Coffee.

A paycheck.

It looks curiously out-of-place in my home, and I cannot stifle a pang of regret at the impersonality of the mail: No jocular, grinning Ray bounding toward my desk and handing me the envelope, signifying Friday at last. No inter-office collective weekend buzz. "Ski, you's got plans?" No happy hour drinks, down the corner, mixing with the blue blazers and their Blackberries, their clean-cuts of self-importance and stock/bond talk, but my gang, crew-like at my back, us, together, assured in our ability not to lose ourselves in the still-strange realm of professionalism. Of adulthood. We showed hints at such things, some of us even considering home ownership. Some of us even dumber. But we were all without the fancy pants. Or the fancy jackets that matched said fancy pants. That time when beer attains that allure, that pre-sex wide-eyed glow of seduction that it can only have for just a few minutes during that end-of-world, end-of-responsibility, hard-work-done Friday afternoon. The hops, batting their lashes: *Ski, take me now... My friends, too!* No one to appreciate my standard payday line: "Stayin' up late tonight..."

And while certainly not my first check for a job somehow less than well done, this was the first for a job, well, not done at all. Not even thought about being done. Not considered for a goddamn second. The past week has been spent chugging coffee on the couch, digging reruns, some Full House here, some Tostito chip crumbs there, a break for porn always just around the corner, between much drawn-out shitting sessions, all in nothing but boxers. The same boxers everyday, actually, now that I think about it. Though I don't think about it. Even the cats, clearly unsettled by their new-found daytime guest, lately seemed to be giving me an inquisitive evil eye.

Don't you have somewheres to be?

...

It Saturday or sumptin'?

And then the both of them, as if in callisthenic warm-up for some kind of off-color synchronized swimming team, collectively go back to leg-in-the-air licking of their own assholes. As if I wasn't even there.

So, sure, it is a sheepish brand of pride as I head to the bank, and sure I deserve a paycheck like I deserve a raise (should I have asked about that in my exit interview? Too late now?). *Hey listen, about this severance and all, it's great, and I really enjoy not being there. But I've been really not there pretty good, for a while now. I've been consistent, and focused in this no-show, no-account regard. So, I was thinking maybe I keep up the not showing up, keep striving, get better at it even, maybe. And I think my past and future effort might be worthy of an increased wage.*

Either way, bankrolled beers, Anchor Steam, and burritos, Mission-style, dance before hungry, jobless eyes. Only a plane and a few hours of sweaty-palmed edge-of-seat leaning lay between Milwaukee and everything else: those hazy golden arches and endless North Beach lattes, my diminutive Chinatown friends making me feel like a linebacker, plucking their one-string, not-quite-guitar-like contraptions on street corners, while I shovel unpronounceable dim sum in my mouth; the nighttime beacon of Alcatraz spinning, nigh as aimlessly as our hero; those old whiskered tourist-trap seals, wheezing and moaning in the after-bar street silence, calling me home.

Uncle Hill – somewhat more attainable on the phone, of the suited sort who's cell is always charged or, who's always in the process of looking, worrying as to the whereabouts for holes for the next charging, unperturbed, mostly, by the flagellations of pituitary cases on a playfield, of the kind to pick up a check, to forget the credit card used to pay said check, but to think it funny, at the next joint, faux-complaining how he'd have to go back in the morning, pulling out a different plastic brand to pay for post-dinner apertifs – is somhow more reliable for plan-making.

The L.A. based shuckster, who works for unions, or against

unions, or something, happens to catch me via cell just days before flight.

"Is this my unemployed nephew?"

"Why, you hirin'?"

"I'd need a resume and some references."

"Motherfucker, you *are* my reference."

"Hmm."

I'm sure's he caught wind through the standard family information aqueducts.

Todd got the boot at work.

What's he gonna do?

Takin' a trip.

Good idea.

The Romans, with their architects and forward-thinking, their much sought flow, would be proud.

"Heard you'll be in California," he asks, conspiratorially, almost-hushed, hinting toward something vile, unspeakable, something to take place in dark-windowed basements, as I picture him sitting, crisp-suited, mustache-trimmed, surrounded by floor-to-ceiling volumes of hard-bound tax law books. Maybe a fire crackling next to his big leather chair. Probably a cat – but not pure of heart, like mine, only purring at twisted thoughts of vulgarity-filled mouse-traps, not even interested in the hunt, just petrified eyes and blood-spurting thyroid sacks.

"In 3 days."

"Hmm."

I can hear the gears working, 30 calculations at once of the kind of mind to puff a J – a white-collar J of fine herb and smoked from a place of esteem and knowing comfort, but a capital-J J nonetheless – and dig "The Paradox of Revolution" before easing into sleep. Meeting times, mileage from LA to SF, train schedules, California topography, the tide, weather, cost, seismic activity, all divided by a numerical value of how badly he might like to see me. There was a formula, always a method, not really comprehensible from the outside, but once that index finger was up under the nose, parallel to the mouth, the back of the second knuckle lightly brushing the sandy 'stache that nobody in the family could remember him without, and you heard the inquiring throaty rumbling *hmm*, from somewhere just below the Adam's apple, it meant he was pulling back into himself for high-minded analysis. Getting his thing together before laying out the cross-examination, closing argument, objection, what have you.

"I got an idea," he starts.

There will certainly be no less than three alternatives and four mitigating factors.

"Yeah," me, half rolling eyes, excited, but none too hopeful.

"I got some meetings in Sacramento."

"Do whatcha wanna. I've got a room in North Beach."

Pause.

"I'm a lawyer, I have 12 suits in my closet. I get my own room."

3

It all seems to be taking a while to get rolling, doesn't it? For that laundry to dry and be wearable. For the ding-ding of microwave job completion. For the cheese to melt in delectable rivulets, ready to run past the wrist and down my forearm. The toast, just refusing to shed that freezer burn, take on toast-like qualities, welcome the butter. With warmth. For the plot to clarify, establish, and spurt forth characters of dynamism, when punchy dialogue flows natural, and there's a clear conflict to be overcome, seen to, worn with focused pride on the lead's armband and worried brow.

But then it comes in something approximating a rush – the smoke detectors blar-blar-ing suddenly, when you thought there was more time to cook.

A 35-mile rush-hour death gauntlet of horns and ass-riding, down I-94, from the parents' suburban Chicago outpost and via American Taxi, no blind-spot checks, cabbie hip to blue-tooth technology and rap-rapping in something vaguely Eastern-ish European, lands me just on time for row 13 on the 10:25 747 out of O'Hare. Like I've places to be. To be seen to: stuff. Pulling the requisite maybe-the-last-words-ever-read lit from the carry-on (here, *The Sun Also Rises*), which also doubles as something of a show-off thing, an identity marker (studious, bitches!, and I'm not even a student!), a thing I can see next to my forthcoming obituary ("the wannabe writer will at least have a spot at that great gin mill in heaven, next to his hero, Hemingway" – the Tribune taking some liberties here), I plop next to a starched, pressed, immaculately uniformed Marine. Or Air Force. Or something of the well-ironed, ready-to-kick-ass world. Barely 19.

"Goin' home?" my fists-up friend immediately inquires, grinning like he's relieved he won't be without company, *a* company – an army thing maybe – obviously one of those not-rare-enough plane conversationalists (maybe it's just the cut of an inoffensive jib? The allure of the side-burned guy into Hemingway and his obvious bag of big, heady emotional stuff) that immediately strike again at a two-kinds-of-people-in-the-world chord.

"Umm."

Exasperated, as if I don't have the time. Head scratching, as if there's too much gravitas. Sucking teeth, like, you wouldn't understand, *man*. Now that my palms are sweaty and I'm too busy pushing through my pre-flight checklist, trying to categorize, alphabetize, figure the last 25 years into 'unsuccessful,' 'almost-not-too-bad,' and 'ehhh' bins of life. Getting my house in order for the inevitable plummet.

But I continue. It's a long flight to be bad neighbors, and already 100 pages in and I can't really tell why I'm reading the poetry-less accounts of no-balls bullfighting enthusiasts.

"Not exactly... You?"

"Yeah. Finally. Leave from training. Been 6 months."

Here we go. With our knees almost touching, my worn cords next to that grandfatherly satin/poly blended, perfectly creased blue, each of us sheepishly vying, feeling one another out for early position on the shared armrest, I can feel a chasm imminent as we both wait for his next, obvious conversation move. Here we go, I think. Only a matter of seconds and all of that rancor, safely and justly stored, all of that venom absorbed, all of that injustice laid upon me by a cruel economy and scheming labor lords, would be pried from my grip and laid bare for everyone in rows 12-14 to plainly see.

Goin' on vacation?

Yeah.

What do you do?

Sleep. Watch Sopranos. Half-hour dumps with the door open have been my bag of late. I'm on to this new site where it's all librarian chicks. Free too. Just got new strings for my guitar…

So, some up-at-6, crew-cut deployee of the Man, because he flew planes that measured speed in Machs, served his country for lengths measured in years, went months without seeing his buddies or girl (nearly librarian-esque based on my furtive glances at his cell phone, no pigtails but we could do something about that), risked life, limb, etc., was unwittingly ready to rob my trip's hard-earned, outsider nobility?

"What is it you do?" he asks, finally, looking up as he turns off his phone, the plane taxiing toward destination or doom, my heart doing that thing where it pronounces itself, forces consciousness of it's existence like at no other waking hour, and you're surprised to see him and ready to placate… *Ah yes old friend, shall we have a drink together?* And a knowing smirk plays at the corner of my new friend's mouth, one implying that he knows my game, knows what I'm up to.

I know your game. I know what you're up to.

Not today I think. Not yet…

"Just retired." Me, feeling good with this answer, ready to ride it, taking a drink of my carry-on caffeine like Grandma does, like it's the one comforting thing at the end of a long life, the conclusion of a fitful night, in and out of dreams of all the many people you've known that died. That haunt you.

"Did you say retarded?"

There's elements that might be true therein, my friend, both in my personal growth, and cognitive capabilities. Oh har har, yes, you hit it, bucko.

"Retired. As in I'm re-tired. Tired. Again."

"Oh yeah?" Him, not knowing, not quite smiling, a bit unsure. Noting my baby-bottom chin that'll always get an "ID?" from even pleasant bouncers. My patchy sideburns seeming pronounced, quite post-pubescent.

But nobody knows me in any of these rows. I glance around, like I'm letting him in on something, take another swill that seems to reek of wisdom, of *man-you'll-never-know…*

"Yep." Self-satisfied, easing back like I fly all the time, no nerves, thank you very much. "Just living off my investments."

Uncle John never had a cell phone, wouldn't be bothered, wouldn't bother. So upon touchdown at SFO, I am to phone his cushy lower East Bay residence, await him to roll across the Dumbarton, up the 101, stop for a pack of Marlboro Reds, pull up in the 'Cab Only' lane, hop out, shift his aviators to the top of his head – a considerable distance on a considerable melon – and finally greet me with that chesty bear hug of an embrace, his 6'4 frame causing immediate emasculation, and somehow rendering me at once less brutish than I saw myself amid the plane packed by crisp suits and Golden Gate t-shirted octogenarians. Taking it upon his own beefy shoulders to load my rucksack of boxers and plaid shirts in the backseat, John wastes time only long enough to snap a picture of me, grinning – caught off-guard – before hopping in and pointing the Saturn's nose north, toward The City.

The towns of Millbrae, San Bruno, even South San Francisco had always been hard for me to justify, contributing nothing but industrial-looking obstacles and distance between myself and what I was so doggedly after. But at the least they offer that we-could-be-anywhere time for post-flight, catch-up small talk. Maneuvering the modest SUV through early afternoon traffic (my Northern California no-job brethren, I think, then remember we're in the capitol of start-up-dom, and freedom here is often associated with massive checks, and people blog for a living, almost like me, but…), for John this discourse takes the form of alternately spouted basketball-flavored non-sequiters ("Jackson been lightin' it up"), San Francisco herself ("hear what their doin' to the Bay Bridge?"), and Mission-style burritos ("You know where we gotta try…"), all while flicking his butt on the window and occasionally sipping from a cup-holdered coffee mug.

Between flapping the chest of my t-shirt – trying to air out the post-flight pit sweat and get a nice congeal before the new city, new trip perspiration takes root – thinking about what the itinerary holds for the night, and doing my best to keep up with John's haven't-seen-you-in-a-year, caffeinated pitter-patter, I'm a bit caught off guard by the 'what are you gonna do now' talk.

So much so that I nearly lose inventory on my healthy stock of ready-made answers when the question does finally arise: "So, what are you gonna do now?" – him, giving a sideways glance while his mouth alternately points the opposite way, emitting a perfect 'O' of smoke out the cracked window into the California sunshine.

Trapped in the gray between half-serious and half-joking modes, I accidentally stumble upon a from-the-heart – at least halfway – reply: "Maybe try ta write a novel?"

I regret the slipped genuineness before the bumbling sentence is even complete. So out of character. I thought I was the tough guy: He, the no-fucks-given afternoon-breakfast-eater, seeking the juice of the *big* questions, not your rote daily uselessnesses, paper-pushers! Who's daily pajama-ed existence is oft-punctuated with from-the-hip philosophes, exclamated at the end with a meaningful "fuckers!" or a hearty, "bitches!"

Though John seems placated, impressed even. I flash on the mystery novels lining his bedroom wall shelves: Lehane, Price, Burke. That type of respectable, gritty literary thing, but alongside mass markets to which my journalism-studying brows would furrow and haughtily heighten, then refuse to even give the time of day: Lescroart, Iles. Was it just me or did they all use the Golden Gate bridge on every book cover? I didn't even have the energy to be condescending in their case, not with my lofty, Hemingway-esque questions to grapple with. But if all of them could do it, make it up there, on the wood of John's homemade shelves, all-caps last names on the spine so prominently, unapologetically facing the world, staring out, pronouncing themselves as publishable, bookstore-able, readable, then maybe there was a chance for my mother's wayward, pen-toting son. The one with the sweaty palms, quarter beard, and half of a half-baked ideology about Kerouac being right about something. About the days stacked against purpose, and that being the very purpose itself. The one currently without a job, wandering toward the most expensive city in the western hemisphere, with a decent room lined up, and, probably, penniless skidrow slumming to be done only between "rye neat"'s at hotel bars. Whatever, fuckers! John's driving, and at least I already knew what I could use on said forthcoming book cover.

Built like a longshoreman (while I've never met or seen an actual working longshoreman, nor do I grasp exactly what they do, I was somehow sure they smoked, laughed, and were mustachioed and forearmed like my father's brother), John is an intimidating mass behind the wheel. Inspiring the sort of passenger confidence usually reserved for professional drivers – despite the random accelerations, mild frustration brewing just under the surface, and cut-offs – Dean Moriarty seems, dominantly, eagerly, on-hand. Better than working I think, snapping a picture of John in my head, and easing back to watch him shift – third, fourth, *vroooom*. I need to learn to do that. Drive stick, or be a man? *Yeah.* I let the dotted lines do their run-the-other-way work. Planes and airports and takeoff tension and the hard parts have come to pass. *Arrived.* Into the sure, hairy-knuckled hands on the wheel. Ahead, the City looms in a haze.

4

Coming from the south – or the east, across the Bay Bridge as in previous, more glorious San Francisco entrances – the first exit can only be the Mission. Rightfully, boldly, no questions asked to the conglomerates of meaty muscle sticking out from the steering wheel, John would have it no other way. Just in case though, the itinerary exists, still crisply folded in my ass-pocket: bullet points under bold lettering, italics properly utilized to delineate names of businesses, addresses with numbers and the nearest-major-street intersections in parentheses, hastily added, pen-scribbled notes in the margins. Any lucky pickpocket, surprised to find three pages of Times New Roman-ed computer paper where my wallet should be, would be graced with a certain, tasteful 3-day route of eating and drinking his way around the City.

Thanks for laying this all out, looks like you know the city really well.
Yeah, well…(blushing).
I mean it.
Um, were you trying to steal my wallet, motherfucker?

The thought of somebody else carrying out my plans is unbearable. Besides, how would I know the proper intersection of Valencia where after-midnight burritos might be located? 24th? 25th!?

"Donde?" "Donde?" Me, wandering Mission Street, perplex and weak-knee with Mexican-like hunger, tears in my eyes and feeling a bit too-cute in my checkered blue shirt, questioning the 16th Street BART station Crips decked in their red (or were they the blue ones?)… "Que, ese?"… Utterly lost, ambling with mouth a-gap and eyes skyward like a Fisherman's Wharf tourist.

Leaning to my left on the seat, I give my right cheek a reassuring pat. Pickpockets be damned – for now.

How to explain 'The Itinerary'? Where did it come from, this need to know every turn, the right name of each street, the mustache-ratings from a random foodie blog, the what-to-order from respective taquerias? Was I scared? Was I lost at some time? Ass-raped at knife-point in a late-night Harlem alley in the '80's? Had I ever had an 'off' meat delivery package anywhere in San Francisco's Mission? All legitimate questions, all basically unanswerable, all asked to myself each time a trip was coming on, even as I sat and perused endlessly and made notes, and pondered and gazed at cartoon Kerouac on my dresser, and figured out the oh-so-perfect passage of road minutes. Distantly, inexplicably, the need is there, somewhere, to not lose a second, to pack it all in.

It's something resembling validation. There's a guy on the TV, and we watch him, the Roommate and I, on run-of-mill Taco Tuesday's, that middling day where it's no longer quite so awful to be alive, with a hangover and smoky regrets, but, maybe new history, where you've settled into the groove and it's way too early to even consider discussing weekend plans – the meat of the ham sandwich of the everyman, pitching-in-to-society, schlubby, nine-to-five life. At least for whom 9-5 resembles something aside from a hockey score gleamed and memorized solely to impress Uncle John. So, back home, the Roommate and I, having recently completed a trip to the grocery store where we did everything possible to disavow any perceived notion of co-domestication ("I'll go over here for the onion, then see ya at the car."), watch the Travel Channel man with the shades and the where-to-go wisdom. To see him explore random U.S. cities – those being the best, the sort of places maybe, maybe we've been – and we see where he drinks, eats. And we beat each other – between greasy ground beef bites – with "I've been there." That place in New York, with the pizza, that joint, in Austin, with the chilli they put fresh jalapenos in, that bar, with the darkness, endless darkness, and Christmas lights, down yonder in New Orleans. Sometimes we're dickish. "Can't believe you've never been to Rosa's. Look at how much fun he's having. You were just *in* Chicago. It's so awesome. You dick!"

It can sting.

One day I'll get there. Next time. And then. Then I'll know. And I'll show everybody. Everybody will see. Ohhhh. How I'll eat that burrito. Fuckerrrrehs!

Now there's a whole gaggle to prove wrong. A gang whose work is currently funding this wanderlust spectacle of boozy drunkenness guised as meaningful travel. But also to show, to prove something to. And the need is there to shout, to brandish. I'll *show you! You don't need me no more? Well I'll eat that burrito that was on TV that one time. Oh, you didn't see that one? Well. I've been there now. Yeah. It was on TV…*

A mountain climbed. A flag stuck in the snow. A picture for the postings upon social media. Strategically dropped upon the world late-ish at night. To really show 'em. In a great prideful parade of hi-def, color, glistening shiny meat grease.

Wow, Teddy's up late. Must be having capital-F FUN!

It's something more though. Just the way the TV man walks, wears his jeans, his shades on inside sometimes and, somehow, not looking like a dick. That casual assuredness. The getting around in some unimaginable place, like Naples, Lisbon, Shangri-something. The whatever-ness of conquering the world. I'd never let on, jamming another beef-on-flour fold into my gullet, ignoring the sadness of our teeny dark shared apartment and the constant Milwaukee need for the radiator clank, but I was always agape at the completeness of said dude's easy life domination. Instead I sit quietly, wait, hope he'll hit a joint in Denver, Detroit, whatever, that I know – just one more notch on my belt. A mild victory. Over the Roommate. Over whatever it was I was supposed to be doing at age mid-20-something.

For now though, no itinerary consultation is necessary. Even fewer words needed. At this point – and most other points during most other days of most other trips, whether it be here, there, Buffalo – John and I are akin souls on a like-minded journey, brothers in fork-wielding arms, the fat fucks you don't want to see coming out of a single stall restaurant bathroom before you. The communicative, unspoken wavelengths of shared ancestry and DNA, not to mention our alike bulbous guts – John patting his own bulge, hairy certainly, subconsciously through his tee-shirt, signifying emptiness – had each of us psychically urging the SUV toward a burrito.

"We're going to Papalote, right?" Me, nonchalantly, namedropping the corner carne asada-slingers that I had been daydreaming of, craving from all the way down in the loin region, salivating over and abstaining from the salty, kind-of-sublime airline peanuts for. Damn near 2,000 miles of soul-leaning toward that weird orange-ish roasted tomato salsa. The other-city-ness of it – no chance at facial recognition, a strange slant to the sidewalk outside, a different murmur in the air, menus, well menus are still menus– but, really, the exoticity all you could ask of an adult-ish life.

"Let's try this place." John, pointing, name-dropping a no-name.

Are you kidding? That's not... I mean, come on. Really? That's not on the... the itinerary at all. It's not even under the 'other possibilities' sub-categories of burrito places... (Flipping through the Word documents). *I don't even know the mustache rating!*

Feeling my blood rise, sensing a wasted validation opportunity, thinking about hitting my ass-pocket for help, sensing the tires on the whole freewheelin' foray coming loose at the axels, the perfectly wrapped burrito actually proven too tight, dribbling black beans through a burst, before I have even, really, started. But I again peep John's forearms on the wheel. Shut my mouth. My poor hungry mouth. Let Dean do his work, I reassure myself. Up and down the hills, right? Though for now, we've only been in the Mission, and the flatness feels under-whelming, somehow insulting to the whole glorious, vindictive undertaking.

We find a parking spot on 18th street, amongst the bustle of grocery cart pushers, plaid-shirted cell-phone talkers, Mexicans on the corner – some squatting, some sitting, all of them giving me the eye – corner stores, hat stores, pork stores, those bay windows. Always with the bay windows. And the parallel running cords overhead that as far as I can ascertain the buses (constantly with the accordion attachments to make them, in fact, 2 buses) filch power from. And everywhere, the yellow.

Calling the Mission colorful was like calling my own block of Milwaukee cream city brick buildings 'not colorful' – obvious, and rightly taken for granted. Looking around I note a sufficient writer could make something big, poetic of the disparity. Different cities like different chances, a downtrodden path behind and sunshine-y horizons, a flight and then new perspective.

Instead, I light up. And amongst some gleaming – fresh, seemingly, somehow – murals of the countless and various plights of Latino Americans – a single glance conveys poverty, AIDS and something about Quetzacoatl – we hit the street. Collective Camels going, John's neighborhood knowledge and formidable girth lend a refreshing swagger, as soon as I slam the door shut and my brown boots contact real City dirt (pavement, whatever) for the first time. It's not unlike something from high school days: making a new friend from the football team, and suddenly strolling the halls, knowingly laughing louder than normal, cockier, chestier, neck more erect in the between-period rush, pimples not such a big deal whilst next to the baddest motherfucker in the class.

It's not quite that John seems all that huge, it is simply his presence that makes everything around him smaller. If 'dwarf' can ever be a verb, John puts it into application. Such is definitely the way with our burritos. Struggling, mouth-ablaze, elbows on the table, manning up as best I know how, ignoring the carne sludge pummeling what is back home an appetite to be reckoned with, alternately dousing each bite of the foil-wrapped monstrosity with red and then green salsa from the tabletop plastic bottles, just putting on appearances, I'm doing my best to keep up. And John is done. Already patting his tit-pocket for the Marlboros and glancing over his shoulder to make an early smoke exit.

"Not bad, huh?" John, doing that thing that done people at a booth do, ironing his shirt with his hand over his gut, reaching down to the seat and adjusting himself back and forth.

- ... Inaudible noises out of a gorged bean hole... –

"How many mustaches would you give this one?"

- ... Nodding, contemplating, blinking, holding up 4 grease-and-verde covered fingers...

One day I think. Pondering steroids, promising myself to continue on the late night bar bell sessions in the bedroom. Always so careful to not let the Roommate hear the self-conscious clink of metal... ("You working out in there, Teddy?" "Nope! Jerking off. I swear. Jerking off!").

Back on the street, having decided on languor, we let the super burritos run their colon-course, leaning, we've got new smokes and a view of the gamut hurrying by: skinny jeans mix with careful presses, high rent imports amidst a few hearty holdovers from barrio days. Mind, slow and satiated, starting to feel in lock-step with John – who claims he's lost only "a dab" of respect, not for the amount eaten (I crushed it, after all), but the time taken – I start to feel that creeping beer-hunger, and consider the rest of the night's looming, glowing potential as I amble in my uncle's formidable pedestrian wake.

A glance at the cell tells me it is 3:30 back home. 3:30 Central Standard Time. Time for the office's UPS pickup.

Teddy it's 3:30, Ted it's 3:30, It's 3:30 Tedd, Ted it's 3:30, 3:30 Ted it's, tedd it's 3:30, 3:30, 3:30, Ted... Teddy! It's 3:30 Ted, it's, Hey Tedd! it's, it's, 3:30, Tedd, 3:30...Ted, Tedd, Teddddehuh...

Extra syllables indicating added aggravation, fuckupedness. The 'Ted' call combining with 'uuuuhhhh' into something closer to 'Teda' than 'Teddy.'

I feel the Rocky Mountains, those jagged, turbulence-causing tits of the great American West, insulating me from all Midwestern-ly bullshit. A bullshit no longer mine. Flushed. A finality for other, less burrito-smeared wrists.

A post-Mexican toot escapes my cheeks and a careless smile dances on almost-always guarded lips. Pausing on the corner of 24th and Valencia, - "this is my favorite part of the Mission." "Me too, me too!" – lifting my cap and swiping my forehead with the back of my wrist, I exhale a plume of smoke and find myself gazing up at John with the kind of sluggish insouciance that recalls what I'd seen once, on the Discovery channel: Sharks, Great Whites, fresh off an endless smorgasboard buffet of whale carcass. Overstuffed and slow, utterly directionless. Bobbing. Like content drunkards. Perfectly, it was just such a scene that had prompted – at least according to the astonished Crocodile-Dundee-sounding narrator – the first-ever filmed Shark erection.

"Shark Boners. Great name for your band," says John.

I didn't realize I'd been thinking aloud.

Later, strong coffee in hand, still strolling somewhere near Balmy Alley's whirlwind of murals and more yellow, the obligatory 'I've-arrived' phone call is yet to be made, and here we're going on a borderline-unacceptable 2 hours post-landing. I thumb to 'Home' and hit dial.

"Where are you, what took so long?"

"I'm in the Mission, mom. And the delay was due to a rape. Might have to testify. But I probably won't get convicted."

"What? Where? Where is that? What's Mission? Where *are* you?"

"Hold on, lemme ask this Mexcian guy."

"No. Don't. Don't ask him if he's wearing red. The gangsters wear red. I heard that."

"Holy shit he's got a red hat. Better wait for a white one."

I picture her tucked away in Chicagoan suburbia, still in work clothes, palms a-sweating over her son. The son, that is, who fancies a living on a per-word basis, who's sitting on a perpetual lottery ticket known as 'severance', and not the one striking $100-an-hour for jazz chording at country club parties. The apprehension over my wanderlust combined with her general unfamiliarity with major American cities always offers prime moments for good-natured panic-mongering. She laughs, generally, nervously, eventually. Harlem, thus far, had really proven the most fun.

"Did you do what you were supposed to before you left?"

"Whaz that?" Me, thumb-and-forefingering out another smoke from my tit pocket, them all going down like it's going out of style, which in California it very much is, which only enhances the general badassery of it all. As does flippantly dogging my mother while flicking my Bic over the Camel and poetically pondering another row of bay windows.

"Did you apply for Unemployment?"

"No need for an application." Me blowing a bit into the mouthpiece, feigning an interfering wind.

"Teddy, don't mess around, you need to apply for Unemployment."

"Mom, I'm *already* on fun-and-enjoyment."

5

North Beach sparkles at night, sure. Like so many postcards of San Francisco – Coit Tower phallic and pronounced in its veiny, ready-to-go protuberance-ness, and the hanging fog so immaculately dreamy, mysterious-like, that Photoshop cannot help but to be suspected. The seals moan, Alcatraz sits brooding, remembering, all out of menace, and the din rises around the bars and grills, and there's a hazy end-of-world possibility in early evening. Like, "where else ya gonna go? There's nothing but water and sleepy death, beyond." And every passed slanted alley holds one million misty mysteries and side doors for end-of-world friends. Sure, yeah, yeah. Yes. There's writers to do that whole thing, maybe paint the clouds a bit too, talk about billowing, and how the fog is ethereal and metaphoric for the pressing ennui of modern Siliconic life. Speak up, poetry-lend the inclines and vistas and cement playground where Joe DiMaggio learned to put his weight into it.

But, clichés aside, little known fact that Anchor Steam actually rolls downhill from Coit's veritable incline, filtering in through the back doors of my various neighborhood watering holes along Stockton, Grant, Columbus. Gravity the reason why my glass never seems to empty. And the bright bulb lights of the titty bars along Broadway are kept aglow not by electricity, but by the ghosts of long snubbed-out roaches – the dead joints of everyone from Kerouac down to me. Dirty Harry too, can be spotted, talking or punching down roof-jumpers, peeping in windows, if you know what back alley to roll down late at night. Bullitt, well, he is over there, riding in the muffler echo roaring over from Montgomery Street.

I know this for I have walked North Beach streets by night. Witnessed it all through glassy, but sure eyes. There's dreaminess and then there's unemployed dreaminess, the difference being that between the fire and the firefly. As a famous writer, who's name I can't recall, once said.

For now though, John and I are hunkered down in a faceless, neighborhood beer joint in Noe Valley. Darkness settling over town as we wrestle with ghosts all our own.

"So, he didn't leave a note?"

"No note."

And I need to find a better answer to this. Something with less gravity than the lowered eyes and head shake that is my only muster. Something with levity. Something aside from 'no note': "You mean, like a track listing – for the funeral?" "There was a note, but it was addressed to his cat, so little Baxter is the only one to have read it." "Yep, but it was in Spanish. And turned out to be, upon translation, just a list of swear words."

So there's something else to that whole hero-becoming posture. Some bit of noble-like overcoming. Some sense of a lead man. There is something else to this venture aside from leisure time and drunk-uncle spats. Beyond the chances to get plowed on Tuesday afternoon's, and pay no mind to the calendar, like a wealthy magnate, there is something else, maybe, upon which the narrator grows and gnaws. Something too much for such early hours; these nascent, barely-sophomoric chapters.

Here we are only delaying my hotel check-in and the inevitable North Beach show of drunken back-patting down the street and shit-eating grins that will ensue till the wee hours. When my throat would be sore with smoke, and John would light a fresh butt from the one he had already burning for the ride back across the bay. North Beach and soon, I think. Picturing The Saloon and its bustling little side alley, biker dudes and other bearded characters lighting fresh joints. A clichéd but capable blues combo blaring the room. "Mustang Sally" and shit, but somehow, here, just this once, I don't mind. The itinerary has already been dented enough and here we were on territory that had been covered, in a diggable neighborhood that still, somehow, wasn't *mine*.

"So you wanna get back on schedule, here?" Me, pandering a bit, to the horse hooves before me on the table, removing my own stick-like forearms back to my side each time I get a perspective glimpse. Or each time the waitress with the smile and tattoo ambles past, with that nose ring and greasy apron, her eyes a promise reservoir of northern California knowingness, of bars and back porches that I could never find with a million of my little itineraries.

But John is still wondering – mouth slightly agape and alternating his sturdy look from my eyes to somewhere behind the left of my head. Paying attention to the hoops on the flatscreen, but only enough to let the water behind his retinas – so I think – subside in the numbing TV-glow of the Madness of March.

"So, he wasn't depressed?" John, taking another substantial swig of Red Hook.

"No depression."

Again, I need something better: "Well, he was friends with me, so whaddya think!?" An elbow to the ribs and a chesty har-har.

Still my reserve is steely. I know its safe discussion ground as long as some froth remains on the pitcher. By the time that's gone though, and the half-full level edges closer – which to John is a signal to start thinking about ordering another – there is no telling the amount of public blubbery that might ensue. And here I was, the rugged Midwesterner in a Kerouac shirt with the Hells Angels-looking dude and his endless Marlboros. In front of an impressible waitress (if she could only see me negotiate the tricky diagonal cut of Columbus Ave, hardly ever confused!). Crying was almost definitely not on *this* itinerary. So I would get through, move on, maintain a clear head for North Beach's supple rolls. Just around the corner. Forward.

"So, how'd he actually do it?"

"A yellow rope."

John sucks down at least 6 ounces with this gulp, clenching and unclenching his fist over the wooden table and softly shaking his head. Feeling a backslide, gripping and lowering my cap, I take as big a swallow as my post-burrito gut might allow, and avoiding eye contact, shaking the table a bit, abruptly stand and make for the door. Mutter something about fresh foggy air. Never knowing what to do when a girl smiles – as my waitress friend is, now, looking up from her book at the end of the bar as I go past – I offer a half-audible 'hi-ah,' in monotone, realize too late it should have been a 'see-ya', and lift the right half of my lips into an awkward puncture of my cheek's roundness. Like some kind of child-molester half-smirk. Smooth indeed, but can't she see that I'm a wealthy magnate?

Did you say magnet?

But I'm over it by the time I push open the door and match a smoke in the now-dark air. Trusting John with the remaining half-pitcher was like asking John Wayne Gacy to watch your first newborn, but I'm over that too.

But I'm your first S.F. pitcher of the trip, don't you wanna take a picture? At least a mental note?

Motherfucker, do I look like a tourist?

I'm already pondering the uniquely San Francisco image of tail-lights disappearing over the crest of a hill, wondering how long this might entertain and distract me as another red pair approaches Church Street's distant crescendo. Probably headed for North Beach.

"Well, there's your book, right?" John, suddenly by my side, jovial, lighting a smoke, referring to the ghost he had just broached, with a glisten of beer still on his 'stache.

"Who said anything about writin' a fucking book?"

In almost silence, I watch John shift and steer us toward San Francisco's northeast corner. Up Guerrero, up Van Ness. The night reaching full darkness along the way. He eventually defers to the 'sorry for bringing up the dead guy' spiel before we turn on Broadway. Me, straight-faced, cutting him off, with bravado: "I'm more sorry that you *desecrated* my itinerary." This, at least, just in time, earns a guffaw and levity more suited to North Beach's approaching bright lights, packs of 20-somethings, and sleaze row – the Roaring 20's! Garden of Eden!

Scuzziness aside, here lays the approach, the landing strip, to my giddy home. John's buzz though, is waning.

"One more?" Me, jocularly elbowing his mammoth right bicep over the armrest.

"*One* more? Him, with a look that clearly implies the gourds of beer that the prominence under the seatbelt could hold. Already did hold.

But the mood has peaked, the leaves are rustling. Burrito shits are to be taken. Bay bridges were made to be crossed. My look is turning outward, anyways, towards the City. And John is making the 'rest until your on the East Bay' excuses. (Smart too, him knowing that any 'gotta get up early' garbage could have been machine-gunned down faster than my half-hearted, 2-year-old resume was about to be at the New York Times. John *never* got up early. For 'nutin.)

He drops me in front of the hotel, a budget job, but with a quaintness factor off the charts. My SF home, my couch-away-from-couch, with ghosts of its own, just up those stairs, just around that corner, just down that hall toward that once-stayed-in room. This time he allows me to shoulder my own load out of the SUV's rear, while he sits at the wheel, steely-eyed and smoking.

"One thing, T." John, elbow on the window, his face dark in the interior, calm with night's-end stoicism, framed by gray smoke like the black-and-white portrait of a '40's jazz musician. Dexter Gordon, or, oh, they all look like Dexter Gordon.

"Yeah?" Me, giddy, armpits pumping liquid, palms too, ready to go...

"You gotta get rid of that fucking itinerary."

And from a quiet strip of Mason Street, I watch his taillights disappear over the top of a hill.

6

"Keep walking, you'll see me leaning out the window."

"Hill, Christ, don't fall."

"Wouldn't be the first time."

"You fall, you die, who's gonna be my reference?"

"I never agreed to be called upon as a reference."

I'm walking down Columbus, negotiating the tricky offshoot tangents of Stockton and then Grant, nursing my solo-night hangover, an eye out for a dangling uncle, staying largely unconfused as Hill gives me directions to his hotel over the phone. ("You'll love this place." And I do, wondering how a big-city, swinging-dick L.A. lawyer with 20-some suits in his closet can usurp me on North Beach quaintness and location… $270 a night is the answer.) Twilight is basking the growing Friday evening North Beach crowds. Tourists and their loose-credit-card lot are packing the Italian restaurants, vying for outdoor seats in the heart of the neighborhood. Black-clad waiters and waitresses bustle with their hand-held torches, setting a candle-lit mood for the overpriced pasta to come. I can't keep track of where one restaurant begins and the previous ends.

"Let yourself in." I do. "Stan's at the front desk, he'll let you right up." And Stan, eyeing me half-suspiciously, setting down his book with extra care like he's prepping for trouble, which instinctively makes me want to give him some, does.

Starting up the roundabout stairs of the Hotel Boheme – with photos of Kerouac, Ginsberg, the rest of my old crew lining the narrow carpeted hallways (I give Jack a serene,'hey bro' nod of knowingness, he gets it. "Sorry about the commodification of your whole thing, comrade." He seems to shrug at this. "Whaddyagonnado?") – I catch a glimpse of my mother's oldest brother grinning, conspiratorially maybe, down from the interior balcony. At least he's inside.

Hill: Gray mustache, most prominently. Striped button-down, naturally. Lanky in a Kareem or McHale all-elbows sort of way, casting an impression of being far rangier than his 6'2 frame. Wiry as John is thick, underlining from first glimpse the disparate forces that must be at war within my conflicted genes. The two kinds of people.

"Christ, Hill. Don't Fall." Me, shouting up to him, my voice bouncing around the old wooden doors of the little boutique job. Pretending to be dizzy, Hill is undulating his arms out at his side in a wavelike motion. Looking faint and leaning from the waist, he is face-first over the rickety banister, leaning on it just a bit, causing a slight creak one story above my head.

"Asshole." Me, assuming the sometimes-necessary, overly burdened father-like tone that only Hill, sometimes a drunken brother, or my cats, can bring about.

Stan, mustached himself, in that 'in charge' official type way, with the furrowed brow of the sort that deal with folks outside themselves – looking to drink, to fuck, to be a boss for a weekend – is eyeing the whole routine over his book with bemused disapproval. His headshake seems subtle, as if to say, to really, resigningly wonder, at us both: "where did I go wrong?" I feel like giving him a piece of my mind: "You only have yourself to blame. You never showed love." Etc. But Hill has already started down the stairs and I at once notice his lips lined red – probably something local, dry, most likely snobbish – as we embrace. Certainly more sinewy than John's bear hug – me getting a sense of both ribcage and an ulna bone – but tight, full of DNA-collision just the same.

"How were the meetings?"

"Ahh. Union magnates."

"Did you say magnets?"

"Magnates. Unions, Teddy. Pay attention."

"Ohh. *Magnates.* Fuckers. Don't even get me started."

We begin up toward his room, forgetting Stan, needing closed doors like 17-year-olds, for disclosure, for further familial *finally-ness*, for drugs. Me trotting behind like the little bro, feeling the armpits begin their expectant drain, a little tug at the heart, before Hill wheels around, unsteady but sure, without hesitation: "Locked out." "What?" "Stan, my good friend, I'll need another key, pronto!" "Certainly, sir."

I marvel at the litigious efficiency, the unchecked decisiveness. It all happening in a second. Impressive considering how many minutes it would have taken me to figure out how to best approach the situation. (*Ok, hold on. Ok, did I check this pocket? Ok, did I check my tit pocket? This tit pocket? Ok, where did I last see it? Let's retrace my steps… Wait.*). Of course I probably wouldn't have locked myself out of the room in the first place.

Hill: "And one more corkscrew."

Stan: "Something wrong with the last one, sir?"

"Not at all, not at all."

"…"

It becomes clear, as I'm back at the front desk, before Stan's high judgment, before I know what's happening, that my responsibility now is toting the backup corkscrew. So I shrug, blush a bit, and take it from Stan while Hill carries the new key – holding it in front of him like a chalice – and leads me, bounding, up one flight, for the second time, to his room. Standing in the now open doorway, I await Hill to return Stan's skeleton copy while surveying the situation at hand. A table is set before an open window overlooking Columbus. With no screen – Oh, Cali, you and your cultural advantages! – the ocean breeze is blowing softly, the wispy curtains billowing and tangoing around the window. Wine bottle: ¾ drained. A computer: Mac Book, the latest, sure. A phone: Apple, also, plugged in. Another wine bottle: full, enticing. Paul Simon waxes nostalgic over the passing years from the tiny computer speakers and I notice a strange Sahara-style netting around the lone bed.

Meanwhile Stan's nasally tenor carries up the stairway from below:

"Sir, I see you have a visitor for the night, perhaps you'd like to hold on to the extra key?"

"What? No. Fuck. No. Nephew! He's my nephew!"

Returning half-exasperated, Hill gives me a mustache-raised smirk, a clasp on the back and a "well, we are in San Francisco…" We settle into the wicker chairs cramped on either side of the table by the window. Now two corkscrews in front of us, at our disposal, we raise glasses – a Central Coast Pinot – and toast the fading Friday daylight of North Beach. Burdened sighs are exhaled. *Finally*'s are released.

"Check out the mosquito net. We can romp all night with little worry of bite on either one of our peckers."

"What the fuck is wrong with you?" Me, offering disgust, stifling a smirk, one I'm told resembles Hill's, one I hope didn't last night when I was dropping smiles all over the neighborhood like a runaway seeking a one-night shack-up.

"You're right, you're right. I don't mind if you bite a little. But don't draw blood!"

Below and beyond us, night is beginning to settle, softly, spreading out toward the far reaches of lofty Russian Hill, snooty Nob Hill, the Mission and John and I's discarded burrito foils. Where were they now? Who had to throw out that garage and where is he? Back in Oakland? Fruitvale? The romance of the yeoman - the end-of-world yeoman and his lucky daily BART trip. Meanwhile the sky is all pink and aglow, a postcard view, again – SF getting a bit show-offy, if you ask me – from a second story perch of the soul. Not how I expected it all to go – the loneliness, the beans, the back alleys, the Tenderloin. I've hardly had to even think about the severance, when it comes, the worry of the balance. The window open, the smoke going ("Stan's gonna be pissed!"), suddenly, we are thrust upon the game: An old sport and a new favorite in nascent adulthood, the sidelines consisting mainly of passed-time, travel, hotels and, most importantly, fresh drinks.

"Cash in that lottery ticket yet?" Hill, tipping an irresponsible glug of vino into my glass.

"Well, now that you're here, old uncle..." Me, suddenly realizing there's cork bits floating, that he hasn't used either of our two corkscrews, that in fact he's pushed the cork down into the bottle with the little springy bar from the bathroom that holds toilet paper rolls – it sitting between us, stained on the table.

"You're looking a little daunted by this, no?" Hill, sensing and deflecting the forthcoming question, broaching the layoff subject with the detached expectancy of a cross-exam, a sprinkle of suspicion, an undertone of levity.

"It's a bit daunting. Yeah, a bit." Me, holding my wine glass by the stem, gazing at it, picturing myself surrounded by smoke billows, the prospect of the poetry of the downtrodden.

"How are you on that other thing?" Hill, here, softens, releases, holds my gaze and drops the sarcastic chip, for a second, though it won't, can't, hold.

"By that... by that, I am daunted." Me, leaning back, half caught in revelry and the unexpected switch in tone, a bit over-romanticized in the idea of me, too, floundering, in the notion of my face in profile, the tortured, jobless writer. The sad beauty of it all. The wisdom that – dammit, has to be – around the corner. The presence of pity, but a chance at bravery, or something, that aforementioned Jodie Foster role, a thing resembling great strength.

I push my plaid sleeves up, hoping for veiny forearms, stiff and unflappable longshoreman stuff, push them down at once, as my uncle eases back, the quaint wicker groaning under his thoughtful weight. His forefinger quickly up under the nose, it's running back and forth through the thick, professorial gray hair. It is a tick, and a familial laughing-point tick at that, signifying alternatives, running calculations, reservations. A single bony forefinger representing the entire methodology behind fatalistic impulse; the wind-up before caustic delivery.

"We can do whatever you want tonight. I'm taking you out."

"Of course."

"Of course."

With this I raise my glass, tinking Hill's, as his random playlist brings about some acoustic early Dead, and two or three hairs go erect, on the back of the neck, while I'm overtaken by California kismet, the limitless possibilities for stumbled-upon corner bars, bottom-less late-night laughs, arms-around-shoulders down the street toward someplace else in the 'Frisco night. And all I care to offer, as the tears begin to well in the corner of my eyes, inflated and glassy with the profundity, irony, my glass held high, is: "to Stan."

"There is one thing though," Hill, smiling, keeping his glass in the air, prolonging the cheers, making sure his is the ultimate toast, the one that counts. "We must remain undaunted."

My gaze holding his, a calm moment passing between us even as the growing giddy frenzy is tugging nerve ends, I promise as much.

"What are the plans after the City?" Hill, back toward reality.

"Maybe become a roofer." Me, not ready.

"I meant your travel plans. And you're afraid of heights."

At the word, with the wine, I'm back toward picturing myself as Jack – Kerouac yes of course, yes, in black-and-white, but, maybe, now I'm thinking London too. Glancing at my new old-looking brown boots, pleased with this fresh possibility: more turn-of-the-century, more loose, less laws, even blacker-and-whiter, equally undaunted with the lot of boxcars, beans, blinds (whatever "blinds" are). Thumbing a ride toward the train. Not buying the ticket, but taking the ride. All shoulders shrugging and devil may care-ing.

"How's your uncle doing?"

"He's an asshole."

"No – the *other* uncle."

"John's great. Big and hairy and great."

"But he won't let you stay with him."

"Who said anything about staying?"

"Why don't you come to L.A.?"

"Eh…" Me, unsure, off-guard, thinking of the itinerary, wary when the cementing stage comes down.

Hill, with a smirk: "You got something better to do?"

7

Now, a half-joint later, night is relentlessly, vehemently taking hold as we exit the Boheme. The vino, beginning to firm a grip, evidenced by my Top Gun-like snap-and-point toward Stan as we pass the desk on the way out. He gives a half-raised eyebrow over his Pynchon, and a proper, life-in-the-service-industry, questioning, "Sir?"

"Thank you, for your wine, Californiaaaaah," crescendoing up at the end, in my best Mick, which is quite good by this point, is my only response, and it earns a congratulatory pat on the back from my uncle as we hit the door. "Good work. Keep the insanity plea in the hip pocket."

I can feel myself growing a bit fearless, to say the least, actually a bit Keith-ish, in the cocksure shadow of Hill. In my blood is pulsing what is maybe near a 200-plus-proof cocktail of red wine buzz, pot, been-too-long companionship, new-place potential and the reminder that nobody on the street knows me for miles in any direction. No risk of embarrassment, no awkward run-ins, little problem with outfit uncertainty, my face can take on that raspberry glow that sometimes follows over-drinking and yet I will hold every bartender's gaze until the drink is poured, change exchanged, and a "thank you" leveled with more big-balled poise than I could *ever* muster back home. Where somebody's judging eyes are always in that nearest dark corner of a too-small town. But it's *now* that I'm home, it having to do with the chemical balance really, though that's neither romantic nor poetic. But it is when I'm chain smoking on Columbus, hand in pocket, head back and forth, nodding all around, every passerby deserving of a "heyya," or "Howyaduehn," smirking, waiting for Hill to run back up to the room to get the forgotten half-joint for later, the prospect of everything accelerating. The need bulges for rooftop bellows, for notice to be served, for some excited Marv Albert play-by-play. ("And Ski, from the top of *hill!*"). Quite the opposite urge of my simple Milwaukee love for cozy interiors, a bedroom full of records, a half pack of Camels and fridge full of cold ones.

Here I am, motherfuckers!

We see you.

Ok, then...Uh... Carry on.

It is, basically, the same warming rivulet I basked in alongside John last night, a flow I've found myself growing nicely accustomed to these past 36 hours; and a strut, I assure myself – every time I go, San Francisco or any of my other little meccas, New Orleans, New York, the hot shots of urban planning, lofty American culture, good fatty food, big dealism – that will transmit back home.

Last night: Beers till dawn, as planned? Not quite, but wine and secretive cigarettes out the window in my impossibly tiny room. With no TV, no phone, no bathroom, faces were made at myself in the mirror over my cup of eight-dollar vino from the corner grocer. Wine glass: one of those shrink-wrapped, plastic 6-ouncers left by room service, filled dangerously high. Wine bottle: due to corkscrew restraints, the cork pushed down within its own grape contents, stabbed actually, repeatedly, until tiny specks of brown were left floating like torpedo wreckage, bounding with S.O.S' between each careless, lip-stained sip. "Desolation Angels" was perused at all the spots of my college-time earmarks; the itinerary was checked, double-checked for today's headliners (Chinatown) and also-rans (Koreatown). All this came after stately solo-beers in Vesuvio, my hat pulled low in the far corner of the bar, postulating and theorizing, that certain smirk rising periodically like the town alcoholic in everywheres, USA. Outlining the two-maybe-three-books-at-once that I would write upon return. At once! Buzzing, positively giddy, over-affable with the bartender and with each new Anchor Steam.

But now, it is tonight, and the bones and graves of all other nights will be ridden over roughshod by the mule and wagon of Hill and Ski. The air as we exit is distinctly San Francisco: At once Cali-warm and Pacific bone-chilling. Heading north – to the sea! To the sea! – we round Green Street and make for Sodini's.

With a full day under my belt, the reality of my vague pilgrimage is beginning to settle – much like the afternoon dim sum of Chinatown in my gut. Plans and explanations are no longer necessary. Planes and airports are now faraway thoughts. Also, for the first time in adulthood traveling memory, on the horizon there is no need for the 'Sick Day' or 'Missed Flight' vacation extension that I had become so, proudly, famous for. ("Missed your flight again, Ski?" Punches in the arm, knowing smiles. "The goddamn snooze button, don't get me started!").

There would be no uncertainty or stomach nerves for that call-in to work. There would be no call. There would be no work. I would stay and search out these ghosts while I left my own to wander the streets of Milwaukee.

You seen Teddy?

Ted who?

Flannel-shirted bastard used to ship?

Oh yeah. Heard he went out West. Or something.

And so I had. Belly-up at the crowded bar of one of North Beach's oldest Italian restaurants. The jovial hostess, with questioning raised eyebrows, had held up two fingers before I took control with a nod toward the bar and a, "No, just drinking tonight." Me, smiling, pleasant, hands in pocket. Sleeves rolled up and buzzed. Like a longshoreman on payday. The main character in my own little novel. Hill, my attorney, trusted friend and hopeful resume-reference at my elbow, like an old dog as a drinking buddy, trying to keep up. Trying to catch-up, despite his head start. "Anchor

Steam, pronto..."

"Hill, I don't think anybody says 'pronto' anymore."

"Nonsense. I won't be daunted by communicative norms."

Before the night ends there will be track deviation: Me, with burrito-necessitating gut headed in a hybrid cab, again, for the Mission; Hill, with the contacts of a Kennedy, or so I imagined, heading somewhere, landing amidst the Nob Hill mansions and lofty social strata that breathed and slept in hotels with names like The Huntington, The Mark. The 'The' clearly capitalized. Proper. While I would be hunkered down, gorging and gorged on al pastor and guac, squatted solo in a greasy formica booth, tuba-pop blaring, the sizzle of the sweaty slab a-going with another order of chorizo, the rapid rap of Spanish, Mexican-looking thugs getting their munchies on. "Ese." "Mehn." Spoken shortly, sternly, sometimes threatening, but not here, not now. Not on Mission Street just after midnight with the grime and hipness congealing into an unhealthy, delicious ball. While Hill, suddenly with snifters of scotch, and suddenly sporting a sport coat, laughed heartily in a leather chair next to a roaring fireplace.

For now though, we're nestled together in the bosom of Friday night Italian food bustle. Our bartender, surely a Jimmy or Tony, has thick black chest hair roaring out from his unbuttoned top button, with forearm hair to match. On his head it's slicked back with the texture and color of Valvoline. His jaw with the severity of a once-OK heavyweight. He is, as they say, on top of shit, this Jimmy or Tony, working the crowd with an easy gangster smile, forearm's rippling up endless martini's, gold chain flapping to and fro through the uninhabitable forest of black chest hair, now glistening a bit, though I try not to look, never mistaking me for being done, always quick with the refill. And Hill and I both are lushly entering our states of respective reckoning, of the silent moments between drunks that one or the other generally, rightfully, out of fear, out of

51

tongue slack, tries to fill. My mind on the road, not the one stretching away from this bar, from my hometown, from my job, but on the path possible for a far more permanent way out. Much further than any flight, even O'Hare, with her catapult capability, spit-like, could have gotten me.

At the point where sensitive drunkenness becomes morbid, I sometimes consider how soon it will be before my own turn to face the devil – waiting in line, nervous, probably not-surprised, how badly my pits will be a-streaming down there.

And you sir, how nicely you've distinguished yourself.

Thank you, your Satanic Majesty. (With a nervous curtsy.)

With all those lofty travels, and the big book ideas too!…

…Devil, are you fucking with me?…

For the time being though, all I can do is pat Hill on the back, order another round, pronto, from Jimmy, or Tony.

8

"I'm on sabbatical."

Me, explaining myself to the chatty cabbie through the murky cobwebs, Aviators and plastic partition of the too-bright backseat Saturday morning. My shoulder is already sore and my pits already doing their faucet-like work from standing in front of the hotel in the sun, holding my rucksack and waiting for a ride as if SF were as on-demand as NYC. It's not, and the aspirin losing pitifully against the hangover doesn't help the processing of this mental culture note.

I've also already spilled fresh, over-strong coffee on the front of my cords, exactly the shape and spot of a pee stain. Actually the look isn't so much of having pissed myself as it is that my schlong has leaked diarrhea, in a perfect dark contrast to my light tan pants.

Mommy, why does that man have shit stains on the front *of his pants?*

Sweetie, that's what unemployed *people look like.*

So begins another chapter in the continuous conundrum of adult life: the best nights, obviously, reliably, painfully leaving the worst mornings. But I keep trying, we all do. As if, in hopes, maybe, that sometime around 30 your body suddenly adapts.

Oooohh, you're doing this to me, again. Oh yes, Oh you. Har-har. Sure, why not. We have such little time left anyhow.

You know something I don't?

And we can collectively go about our scotch-y late nights by fire places, with books, chess or something, what those old fucks do – and still wake up with the butt crack of dawn. To go to church, chop wood, make tea, whatever.

But now, as if leaving San Francisco weren't already hard enough, as if a sad 'so long' to another not-gonna-say-this-but-no-clue-when-I'll-see-you-again uncle weren't enough emotional baggage in and of itself, as if a post-Hill hangover wasn't bad, in a piercing cortex-fuck manner, somehow I've found myself attempting to make a cabbie understand how I've earned a genius grant, what that entails, and just what I'm up to out here on the Coast.

"Like I said, *sa-bbat-i-cal*." Enunciating each syllable as if it were its own word, aloof, professorial with the indignant air of somebody sick of stooping to explain himself to all these fucking peasants. I had learned to ape my turtle-necked college English teachers rather well, had been practicing the eye-roll since even before graduation.

"But what's the *idea*?"

Good question, buddy. "It's a three-parter. About an adventurer, trying to find himself. Reconciling limitations. Set to music. Really, it's a period piece."

Instructing the private investigator-slash-literary critic behind the wheel to the nearest BART station, "pronto", I was hoping to lay my throbbing bean back, sing the appropriate Tom Waits leaving song in a sad inner voice, pop another aspirin, root for it to get down there and get to work, and wistfully gaze at the fading San Francisco scenery. Now noting how different, more droopy, less hopeful the passing hills, coffee shops and overhanging cables all seemed than on my first day with John. Wondering what I always do upon any departure. Wondering how everyone gets to stay. What gives them the right as an unloving cab pulls me toward a plane and back toward rudimentary existence? Wondering more so now that terminations and endings suddenly seemed such a recurring theme: Does all this still exist even after I leave? Does City Lights still maintain that same smell, even on some random Tuesday, when I'm in Milwaukee? Of course. How do I *know*?

"So. Does he do it?"

"Huh?"

"Does your man find himself?"

"I don't want to ruin it for you."

Side note for a novel idea: A bit of participatory journalism chronicling my character adventures in the back seats of cabs. Sometimes I get into cabs with resounding vociferousness ("How ya doin,' my Man!"). I don't know why. Other times I act annoyed, like a busy professional short on time and long on places to be ("No, no. Take 8th Avenue!"). Just to see what it feels like. Sometimes I go along with blatant racism, sexism or the driver's otherwise cabbie-centrism ("Yeah, yeah, take a look at *that* one!"). Because I can. Depending on my place, mood, level of sobriety, and the overall vibe of the backseat, I've always considered cabs a dressing room for the personalities I've never bought, taken home and broken-in.

As usual, the nostalgia of goodbye irks a literary spark, so I make a mental note to set it down later, in long, passionate, high-minded and calculated prose. But any serious intellectual work will have to wait. At the very least until the aspirin punches in for the day.

Last night, after our respective scotch snifters and super burritos, Hill and I had rendezvoused at his hotel: "We'll rendevous at the hotel." "Rendevous? Sounds a little gay, no?" "If you think that's gay, wait 'till you see what I have on!" "Can we invite Stan?" "Couldn't call it a rendezvous without Stan!"

Wine bottles were opened ("No, no, try *this* screw"), eyes were glazed, joints were rolled and smoked on a short jaunt up Kearny toward glowing Coit. End of night over-emotion and weed tenderness were beat back with tough, manly swallows and throat-clears, but just barely. And not before, at one singularly picturesque intersection, the neighborhood still and quiet around us, the bay windows dark overhead, Hill took time to stop, put a wiry hand on my back and utter, "I'm really sorry about your friend."

Back in his room: "We'll drink till 4 and fuck breakfast."

"Hill, actually, on the itinerary…"

"Fuck the itinerary."

And so we had.

Hard. Right up the ass. With a wine bottle. My carefully crafted regime sodomized by two miscreants beyond lost in the throes of nocturnal revelry. Our cig ashes messily blowing around on the table, our laughter unrestrained, uncaring, spilling out the open window on the cooling North Beach night air. Stan's name was by now evoking schoolgirl laughter at the end of seemingly every other sentence. I was leaning forward, getting up and exclamation-pointing sentences with a forefinger leveled at Hill's chest. Remember-When's dominated alongside declarations of musical favorites and other bleary-eyed convictions.

Later, slouching alone back toward my hotel, sometime after four, I had the image of myself in the grainy black and white façade that everything in the 50's looks like: checkered plaid shirt, clever cap, sideburns, the smoke wafting from the corner of my mouth, a piano's sad chords scratchy and barely-audible. My stumble was stuporous but knowing, beleaguered, slightly beaten but grinning. Like a longshoreman, all work boots and chest, unfazed by the futility of a strike (whatever it is they do, there had to have been a strike somewhere along the way, right?). I could hear the seals moaning low in the not-too-distance. And here I was again, left alone, by another town closed too early. Out of drink, minus a job... 'Another goodbye to another good friend' echoing, Hill's image big and engrained, provoking another solo smile as I wondered on whether or not he'd finish that last bottle, shaking my head – the sad, now alone badass of lonely, late North Beach nights.

At the corner of Columbus and Mason, rounding the way for home, in front of the North Beach Library, I spotted a green steel trashcan, with the block letters: 'San Francisco Recycles.'

Indeed.

Without breaking stumbly stride toward my hotel, with only a quick pause to reach into the ass pocket, I pulled it out. Sensing this as one of those moments, maybe of more to come, that requires hard thinking about not over-thinking, action and not adjective, swilling and not smelling, I dropped in the itinerary.

9

The cell phone has never worked from the bottom of San Francisco Bay, never shown even a flicker of life. Yet I continue to try. Every time, conversation fully prepared, expectant and ready to talk, giddy with conversation-hope like rarely else, my thumb doing its instinctive work of seeking out the green ('go phone, GO!') 'Send' button. Of course by now, the reality of what I'm sure is miles of murky ocean water pressing above my head, along with the concrete tunneling and quake-proof tin can tubing that ensconces me should probably precede any expectation of cellular signal penetration. Maybe they got new towers. Maybe if you call in the shallow part. Maybe, I don't know – *technology*. That certain irrationality, boneheadedness, of travel, can sometimes be pervasive.

It's the same illogicality that causes five-page Word documents with six-to-ten food alternatives for every meal of a forthcoming trip. The same absurdity who's drunken cousin allows one to trash such a thorough life-advisor. The approximate general stupidity (at least when viewed from the easy chair of at-home hindsight, where everything is logical, sober, slow), that makes $10 tips to cab drivers not only reasonable, but sometimes, absolutely necessary (yet another backseat personality: Unemployed Moneybags).

So here I am, BART-barreling toward the sun-kissed, funky East Bay, Moto flipped open on my lap, again surprised and mildly disappointed by the 'no bars.' Obsessed with the ideological awesomeness of a cross-country, from-the-bottom-of-the-San Francisco Bay cell phone call to my brother (Marv Albert, again: "Ski, from the bottom of the Bay!"). For the simple, stupid-grin question of, "guess, where I'm calling from?"

But instead my only Scuba-level conversation is a one-sided

bout with the gray-bearded burnout who got on at Embarcadero. With his requisite beanie-type cap (even a No-Cal acolyte grows weary of such artifacts by day three), guitar strapped on back, battered racing bike at side, he's standing by the door and babbling sub-coherently to anyone within earshot, to the window itself.

Me, mostly just nodding and grinning.

My emaciated former-hippie friend: "they want to limit the definition of marriage to that between a man and woman? What then of the love between a boy and his bong?"

Still, no bars. And the only thing keeping me out of a full-blown repartee with the kook is constant glances at the painted facsimile of the Bay above the train doors. Avoid eye contact, look up, look at the phone, repeat: the practiced rigmarole of public transport users in cities where communal sanity level is anything but static. And there's the image: with the City looking like the West Coast's engorged penis, jutting out into the lapping waters of the Ocean, its not much of a leap to see the Bart's multi-colored lines on the map as the pulsing Johnson-veins of the entire peninsula, pumping and carrying to and fro. Me, the blood being pulsed toward the tip, have my eyes glued on the dot labeled 'Fruitvale.' Counting the stops, racing toward ejaculation, premature though it may be. I'm remembering Uncle John's instructions, picturing him hunched, waiting behind the wheel in the parking lot, patting his gut, checking his wristwatch like people without cell phones still do. But most vividly, I'm seeing the taco shops before us, somehow foreign and somehow east bay-ish – blacker, greasier, beanier maybe? – as light breaks through the windows.

We emerge from the Bay, my heart turning away from departing-despair and toward new-city, new-kicks palpitations – *ahh, smell the air, Sal!* – or something, it seeming almost tired by now, even for this semi-worn but still-excited schlub, now pulsing with the obligatory new-place pit-and-palm sweat. Oakland: previously un-plundered bounty of strange impoverished blackness, gray urban wasteland of what I'm told is comparative and surprising sunniness. Homeland of Jack, London again this time, and treacherous, miserable gridiron fans.

The wild man continues, now staring out the windows with a distant look in his eye, as if communing with the far-off Oakland hills through their hanging gray fog shroud. Vamping and expounding on the earlier theme, more subdued, almost under his breathe: "What then of the love between a man and his guitar?"

With my mind now bounding between burritos and San Francisco-as-penis metaphors, I see myself again, the perspective of between-places, miles-from-home traveling: the blood of John, and all his contrarian anti-technology beer swell; the nephew of Hill, and all those pressed, tallied suits; all of us, in our own way, maybe, somewhat, normal in the end.

This guy, well, this guy is just fucking nuts.

By the time we're cruising the various degrees of grime on International Boulevard – the taquerias, fruit stands and Tecate-signed bars, me sipping on a Jarritos, John negotiating the half hoopty/half pimped-SUV traffic – my bowels are protesting their first stages of we-didn't-sign-up-for-this work on the steak chile verde burrito. John, naturally, is unfazed, easing digestion with a Marlboro, nonchalantly narrating the passing world of decay and grit through plumes of left-handed smoke. Rain is tinkling on the windshield, and through the marked absence of money, excitement, and gentrification that embodied our last drive, I feel like I'm riding shotgun in some kind of detective noir bit. As if Dashiel Hammet's San Francisco, now so hidden, has actually sprung forth once more, has followed my BART train to set up across the Bay.

I consider broaching the subject of who would play the Fat Man, reaching over to pat his seat-belted protuberance, but John is strangely serious, focused. "This is what I gotta show you," he says, flicking the butt against his water-dotted window, turning onto Foothill Boulevard. Three doors down, next to a bacon-fat-greasy body shop, and across from a just-as-delicious-looking Mexican joint, I see a locale straight off of my back home book shelf: 'Hells Angels M/C Oakland.'

At least so it says in massive red-lettering, but John's already parking the car and getting out like he wants to verify. Or like he's got a fucking appointment. "We'll see if Sonny's home," I hear him mutter, slamming his door and moving across the street, an Escalade slowing to let him cross. Not knowing what to do, I get out and begin to follow, only realizing after the door is closed and locked behind me that John isn't moving toward the building, but toward three dudes – Fuzzy, Moldy, Cisco - I just know, *know* their names to be, or to be like, and a slim, mostly-cashed, maybe at-one-time half-hot, Mexican-looking girl. Me, trying to remember Hunter's depictions of gangbangs and other libraried Angels information that I knew, just *knew,* might come in handy one day. Mostly trying to reason away how bad a chain whipping might really hurt. But John is moving toward them, actually *quickening* his pace like a man toward a curbside cab he's afraid is about to pull away. The fellas, lady passive in tow, are making for a beat-up Civic parked in front of the bland brick structure.

"Hey can I just get a picture of my nephew and you fellas?" John, still ten feet away, shit-eating grin crossing his face like he's an Asian tourist at the Golden Gate Bridge. The ones with the hats and the cameras and the rain coats. So happy. So arrived.

"What?" The leader, Fuzzy, all tattoos, kinky gray beard, black leather jacket and beer gut approaching bowling ball proportions but in a somehow badass way, seems taken. The definition of incredulous.

"Yeah, my nephew here's from Milwaukee..." John, as if that explained something about his forwardness. His comfort and unabashedness. Or the need to get a picture.

Me, cowering behind, but it all happening like a car wreck, simultaneously too fast and too slow. I find myself crossing my arms. Wishing I had done more curls back home before the trip, wishing I had left the plaid back in the City, wishing I had stayed in the car.

"No fucking pictures, my man," says Fuzz, or maybe it's Big Al, leveling a nubby index finger in the general direction of John's chest, which is a good six inches higher than Al's own.

John, silent, a laugh tugging at the corners of his mouth, raises his camera playfully, before letting it drop by the cord around his wrist and holding out both palms in good-natured surrender.

"Listen, there are some guys in there, watching you, any pictures, and there's gonna be a fucking problem."

"Sounds good," John, smirking, placating, sounding like a father that has just been reprimanded by Junior for buying the wrong cookie brand. He backs off two steps and watches the posse enter the car with an amused look. I feel the relief wash over me, even a smile begin to tug at my own lips, my chest pumps a bit, before I see John lean back in toward the car.

"Can you just do me a favor?"

Glares meet his eyes, part fuming, part aghast, not only is this civilian *talking* to them, but actually bending over, his considerable bean is nearly in the car now, and he's resting forearms on the open window like you might to a next door neighbor over a fence.

"Can you please, if you don't mind, just say hi to Sonny for me?"

Without a word, the Civic peels out, certainly and obviously speeding toward what will be, now, a rather furious gangbang.

"That was a bit nuts, John. Fuck." Me, back in the car, half-smiling now after a hasty picture – arms crossed, all badass – by the front door, wiping my forehead with a goosebumped forearm of red plaid.

"What?"

But John is already lighting a fresh smoke, pulling away, pointing the nose of the SUV toward the second of his favorite Oakland hoods. Giving me a questioning look before his eyes brighten suddenly with something forgotten. Like he meant to ask how a recent job interview went, how a new relationship was going, or how good was an untried taqueria. The normal questioning expectance between family members over state of the union matters.

And he asks, as he hits the gas: "Hey! Did you try a call from the bottom of the Bay?"

10

Up and down Telegraph, up and down College, 'no bars' has assumed new pervasive meaning. Carousing Berkeley began leisurely and languorously, buoyed by Uncle John's send-off herbal gift and only a notion of creeping thirst. Now though, devolving over the course of hours and a budding traveler's chappedness between my legs, that dryness has become a half-depraved, fully-desperate scrounge for a stool, some chest-height wood for laying my elbows, and any amount of distance between my person and all things so scholarly and ambitious.

Even the Berkeley hoboes have a studious slant.

"Any idea where I can get a drink?" Me, shoulders shrugging, frustrated but chummy after a long hour avoiding panhandlers and apparently missing any watering hole on Telegraph.

"Hhm." A black dude in ratty Raiders hoodie, rattling garbage bag tossed over his left shoulder, right forefinger and thumb to his natty dark chin, eyes gazing off to the upper right as if he were trying to remember some Hamlet stanza of yesteryear. "Maybe a bar?"

Touche. And I'm charmed. I imagine finding an alley, back by the dumpsters behind the physics building perhaps, a bottle of Thunderbird passing between the two of us, that over-compensating phallic symbol in the middle of campus blearily but barely visible in the distance where the studious Asians are bustling by with backpacks full of books of marketing strategies, phones full of pretty-girl texts and social media-aimed pics, bananas, or granola, or whatever it is that keeps them so skinny, so bright-eyed. This guy though, telling me the secrets of my own life as filtered through the failures of his, enunciating and pointing wild in his finger-less gloves. "So you see? So you see!?" Us, finally forgetting it all, slurping the bottle's dregs and sitting back against the building, resting our wrists on our knees as it gets dark, beginning to count his garbage-bagged cans of coke, students' for sure, used for all-nighters that are far from the fun kind, plotting where we can cash them all in and re-up in a grand way. Splurging this time, a bottle of Night Train, some Kools and a seat on some other side grass with a view of the darkening Oakland hills.

In truth though, before any such street union is the need to pee. Coffee bars have usurped every corner in town, and though I'm an aspiring hobo, the quality-caffeine jones is near defenseless in the face of Peets, and my bladder now protests, moans, stretches with each step. The unfamiliarity, the feet fatigue, the *lookatdat* excitement – all passed, ruined by the oldest of back home notions.

As I wander away from the Raiders fan and through the alternating concrete and woods of the made-for-catalog-covers campus, trying not to gaze up at that monstrous tower, whatever it is, least I be discovered as a gawker, and non-student, I try each academic building. I start with one with an Asian sounding name. Locked. Head down, unwavering, 'damn I forgot my key card, har-har,' I head toward Chemistry. No dice. 'Oh man, I'm such a red-faced freshman.' The math building? No give. Life Sciences? What's more science of life than my dick dribbling uric acid? Nothing, but nothing doing with the door. *Look, I know I couldn't go to school here, couldn't even put it on my 'stretch' list with a straight face, I know I'm a B student with no community service type sweeteners, I know journalism degrees are for lazy stoner dreamers who just found out about Hunter and think it sounds part sexy while it also won't necessitate a cutdown on drinking, I know when I look at the pretty young Asians it's in more of a creepy townie kind of way, even though I'm not a townie, and even though being a townie here sounds like a nice warm dream to me, and I know I'm not even capable of gainful employment, couldn't even hold down a shipping-slash-paper-sorting-and-straightening position in an anonomy-*

ous Midwestern town. But please, given the difficulty of my plight and the current economic climate, the dignity of a flushable toilet? Maybe just a hole?

Fuck it. I find a tree off a beaten path and whip it out. Feeling diseased by degrees, but vindictive. In the brush I gaze unflinching at the tower, Sather Tower, I'll find out later, but who cares? And my manhood shoots free.

By the corner of College and Ashby, as yet another potential bar-sighting turns out to be yet another vegan/veggie/bullshit tree-hugging atrocity of fruit drinks or otherwise unhelpful libations, I spot, again, a kindred spirit.

"New student, bro?" He asks after my drink inquiry, unequivocal about the crusted gob hanging from his middle flap of nose skin that gives us a left and right nostril – as opposed to one magnanimous breathing hole.

"Not exactly."

"Ahh, a working man…?"

"I don't want to get into all that."

You see, friend, there are actually more than two kinds of people in the world.

That's what the other kind's always say…

In my head, this is about the point I nonchalantly pull up my shirt sleeves, subconsciously expose the tat as I hand roll a cigarette. Said tat: An engorged green-ink bald eagle, red dripping from his chin, cigarette protruding from the mouth, a stick of dynamite in one taloned claw, a severed, bleeding tit in the other. It's only half visible due to the forest of curly black on my forearm.

"Just happy to be outta jail."

"Ah." Him, looking at me sheepishly, maybe taking a half-step back.

"Whaddya gonna do now?"

"Smoke this cigarette." Me, pensively, Eastwood-ish, a half-scowl, deep and effected, or is it affected? Almost grimacing as plumes billow about me and the man, who has seen some shit, who has hitchhiked and picked up hitchers, who once saw a moose on a hike in Alaska, whose brother ran away and joined a traveling circus as a ride-setter-upper, can only look on with befuddled curiosity at the shadowy figure before him.

In reality, my sleeves are already up, the sparse hair and wispy hints of veins exposed. I offer him a Camel, shrug, and head west. For a second I flash on my pocket contents, not the wallet or my apartment keys (don't they seem so futile, so benign 2,000 miles from home? Or isn't there work for them here too, somewhere?), but on the one-hitter and rolled up plastic baggie of Uncle John-herb. Maybe me and this one, we could find an abandoned car, a bus, or God-willing, one of those flaming garbage cans to sit around. So comforting, heartening, as we warm our hands. Tell 'em about when I got gonorrhea from a boxcar in Montana as he hands me back the little pipe. Him with a story of killing a scab during a railroad strike as I puff... Instead I find myself solo again, looping back toward Telegraph.

By the time I hit campus, undershirt crusted with loopty-loop saunter sweat, flannel soaked through too, weary and parched, about to spark some of John's going-away present for a lift, I've settled on the 10:12 to Seattle. No more Berkeley, no more hesitation, no more major universities, I assure myself, a contemplative finger up under my nose, pissed and sore and *done*, content in decisiveness. And then, near the exact moment of decision, next to a hotel for prospective parents in between tours and their attempt to decide whether or not to send Junior here for a 100K-plus 4-year-vacation of overpriced pot and cheap beer and experiments with homosexuality and conceited aloofness-getting, snuggled between Telegraph and College's main drag, a Sierra Nevada neon light is, finally, calling me home.

I sit, pleased beyond measure, actually give myself a 'good work' pat on the chest, and then hunker with both palms down on the bar, a sweating Red Hook between. Before I realize the ruination around me.

Of all things to happen at a drinking establishment, of all the gin joints in all the world to stumble upon, of all the bullshit I've witnessed at all the various watering holes of my road, a game of team trivia is raging behind me. Young heads are huddling together around tables, conspiratorially, giggly, with in-love-with-knowledge, edge-of-seat leaning toward the next question. As if whoever hears it first has the best chance. As if every front row hand-raiser from every grade of my 18-year B-is-fine career has found their spot. Perfect I think. Fucking perfect. Feeling detached, absent-mindedly flipping through the show-off beer list, dodging the bartender's confused, pitying looks that are trying to peg me, utterly alone now, again, I think of my guitar strings growing dust, accumulating cat hair back home. I think about John and Hill, already back at their own version of home, already back to work (well, maybe not in John's case, and Hill, ever ready for interrogation, mustache-irking conflict, never, completely, ever really stops). I think about my workmates, former workmates – pardon – currently pushing off after a grumpy, sleepy Monday, levity rising in the day's growing shadows. Maybe hitting Jimmy's for some pick-up beers. Maybe some friendly games of pool or darts. Me, never wanting to play generally, but the beer eventually, always putting that fire in the belly, growing me fierce. And I can see them there, racking up, chalking the tip of a new night.

Office sure runs smooth without Ski around.

Who?

Har Har...

After three or four, enough to assuage the growing trepidation of just how many miles and states lay between me and Seattle, the bartender, happy to offer mercy, calls me a cab. Stumbling outside, I feel like the last day of high school, condescending in my indifferent, ignorant coolness.

On to bigger and better things, motherfuckers!
Oh yeah? Like…?
(crickets).

I can see myself, nonchalantly ambling past a struggling team at one of the bar's many circular tables, their head's in consternation, paying me no mind as I stop, lean forward, gently lower my head and whisper "it's lime." "Huh?," guffaws, them barely looking up, bothered, but me following through: "Lime. What gangsters use to cover dead body scent. The answer to this question is Lime." And then I keep walking, and the girl, a tiny thing with flowing hair and the future whatever she wants it to be, a Junior from small town Iowa studying chemistry but contemplating law, she'll look up, her eyes batting magnificently, amazed, gazing at my back as I saunter through the door, her boyfriend, with combed blonde hair, on the crew team obviously, outraged, indignant. Or maybe, instead, as I exit past a table all a-lean together, whispering thoughts and convictions in hushed, glorious intelligence, I'll stop, grip an Asian boy's head in each of my sure palms, and bring them together in a thunderous clap of skull devastation… But now I'm forgetting what kind of character this is, this leading man, and I'm losing grip even on the type of flick.

So simply, for the last time, I wander outside into the cool California night.

Settling in, I'm thankful to plop my over-walked, scabby underscrotum in the plush backseat, my rucksack beside me. Grateful that the cabbie seems so much less pesky than the degrees, professorial beards, and self-conscious glasses that have been in my face since stepping out of John's car. He's relating an everyman's tale of a North African immigrant, driving a cab and living in North Berkeley, the road and his voice comforting me as we head to the train station over in Emeryville. Even though I can hardly decipher a word of his broken, Caribbean-ish sounding English, or hear much over the pulsing Nigerian funk that I don't think to ask him to turn down.

"Ride for free," he seems to keep reiterating, talking about his life, and growing giddy, I can't help but to nod along, ready to dig the riffs the wheels might knock out, on my way to half-drunk.

"And you, you have a ride for free." His voice going up a bit at the end, giving me a half-glance like maybe it's a question. But I'm mostly just nodding dumbly, thinking maybe it's the refrain of the song. Starting to groove now, seeing the road opening up before me, thinking maybe it's some kind of African proverb. And it *almost* goes with the music. Bobbing my head, feeling it, I can't help but sing along, suddenly and righteously finding the refrain for the whole journey. 'Ride for free, ride for free…' And I'm unsure why I'm going to Seattle and not South, to L.A., but yeah, cool, Jimi, ya know, cool.

Dreamy, the driver too seems to vibe on it, as if he were waiting for just the right passenger to you know, *get it*. And that's me, *motherfuckers*. Maybe there's hope for this town yet.

But something rings just a bit differently the last time I hear him say it. And it's only after slamming the door, after leaving his smiling face with a near 100% tip ("really, man?" the emphasis in all the wrong places), does it occur to me.

Ride For Free wasn't that at all. It was letters: P.H.D.

This grooving brother, the serendipitous negotiator of vibes and traffic, so rife with African juju, steering me back toward the road and myself, was discussing, practically, reasonably, academically, the attainment of a PhD.

11

There are certainly writers who can describe what unfolds out the windows of the Coast Starlight train, just after daybreak, halfway between the Bay and Seattle, somewhere in the nether region where the distinction between California and Oregon blurs into a gelatinous mess of brown, orange, and then later, white, white, and white. There are proper, descriptive terms and their users. There are those schooled in geology, geography, whatever the fuck. Mapmakers and globemakers, too, with knowledge of names, who know how to accurately design those basketball-sized spinning worlds with their bubbling topographic corpuscles jutting out, always irresistible to my greasy mitts as a kid, feeling so much like burned skin bubbling up. There are scribes of naturalism (or was it realism?) of the timelessness of mountains, trees. Poets of the breeze and what it all means.

I am not that writer. In fact, I don't even know the name for the type of snow-covered trees emergent in a distance endless out the window, as the Amtrak snakes back and forth and up and then down on what I will later come to know as 'The Cascades.' Actually all I can relate to is the snow itself – deep, forever-looking snow that knew no Spring. Spring and the Sun and Warmth and all those fellas seemed to somehow owe this vast whiteness some money: I could tell none of 'em had or would be around for a while. And the way it bogged and piled, hung upon the defenseless branches, pushing and weighing. I somehow flash on the role of a tree in a hanging...

Geez, ya know, all I'm doing is standing here, ya know, swayin', mindin' my own business, ya know, maybe drop a few acorns, but, no big deal, ya know? Now look here, look at this whole mess I'm mixed up in here...

"What are these mountains?" A woman across the aisle, in a greasy Missouri hoodie, yawning and waking in the orange morning light, traveling alone and obviously a fellow ignorant Midwesterner.

"Yes, I believe so. Mountains."

"But, what mountains *are* they?" Rolling her head, working out the neck kinks that come from a train designer somewhere, at one point, deciding, 'naw, they don't need to recline *all* the way.'

"Sorry, never studied gastronomy." Me, with a smirk, trying not to be pissed that I have to unlodge the nubs in my earlobe to answer her. Nubs mildly painful, but bearable and even pleasant while blasting out every conceivable train song known in modern music. Feeling quite satisfied with myself and how far I am. Away. Feeling sorry for these idiots reclined, dozing around me, without the foresight or care to plan a lengthy playlist of songs dealing with the current task at hand, the present view, the rails.

Some men searching for the holy grail...

Singing loudly in my head, as I do. Moved to tears, almost, by the Tom Waits, as I also do whenever the first layers of *real* travel begin to wash over me in a train seat – or maybe, if aided by Xanax, a plane seat. Relishing the distance, the miles, the romantic nomadicism that seems to pulse from the loins anytime weekend momentum carries me thusly off the couch. And where was my couch now? 2,000 miles away. I can almost not remember her sweet red contours, her knowing ass-groove, that whole other groove I forget until laying down, in just that right position, and *there it is*. Almost. The beginning of a wander is such, like the first layer of movie popcorn, so hot, glistening, promising. But inevitably the reality of an over-priced tub of cooling air kernels will take hold. After all, this was damn near a 24-hour ride.

But for now, after a near-drunk 5 hours through the dark in the fetal position, now coming to life with a piping hot cup of joe and some freshly-bought Ferlinghetti on the seatback tray in front of me, with my digitized playlist of old-timey hobo shit pulsing in the inner ear, and the Earth's multitude of jagged, malignant tits spectacularly reaching for the heavens in the window's growing daylight, it is easy to feel good. For now.

But there ain't nothin' sweeter than ridin' the rail...

For I'm presently so removed from the future or past that there's really no other place to be. I would guess Oregon, but I'm not even completely sure of my present State. I'm so far removed from what day it is, in fact, that I can't completely recall when it was that I found myself bleary-eyed, half-stoned on some secretive hits of Uncle John's herb, stumbling into the Emeryville train station restrooms, only to be paralyzed, suddenly caught between the euphoria/paranoia paradox of potheads everywhere, by the sight of two cops, dongs-in-hands at the pissers. Them, giving simultaneous half-glances over broad shoulders, smiling at the embarrassing awkwardness of the situation. Having no idea how amplified the gracelessness by my stony state of mind. Having no idea how little I wanted to go to jail, for the 1/8, right there in my front pocket, not even hidden, not even pushed all the way *down* with the lint. And, as is the universal unspoken agreement amongst fly-down men, there was a one urinal buffer between the two, and now, it was obviously my only place to slip in. Thinking: I could back out, but that would be highly suspicious. I could head to a stall, but, shit, what if I have to kick up the toilet seat? What if the upward motion of my person kicking up the toilet seat causes the unhidden pot bag to tumble backwards, out, where it will clearly roll nowhere but under the stall divider and be there, plain and obvious for the cop to see. Their easiest drug arrest ever, one for the books, for the racketball courts and policemen's balls. *You believe that little stoner? And all because he's so afraid of toilet seat germs on his hand.* Pot paranoia gets me that far ahead, to the point where these two beefcakes are 'member when-ing with beers around a picnic table while their off-spring, the future enforcers, frighteners, bullies of the world, play at their sandal-ed feet. So, like so many challenges in life, I decided to meet this one with head down, eyes on the urinal cake.

"This will be the safest piss you ever took." One of the cops, giving Pete a good, long shake, seemingly savoring the moment. Relishing his broad-shouldered protectiveness of society, literally cocksure in this little bathroom.

Har-Har.

"Maybe. Or maybe I'll get arrested for this concealed weapon here in my pants."

Har-Har-Har-Har.

Blushing, a bit, my heart is beating like I'm unzipping in a completely different situation.

"Where ya headed?" The other cop, wanting to get in on my non-threatening, slight-shouldered charm.

"I'm not sayin' nothing without my lawyer present."

Har-Har.

"What is it you do, fella?" Cop #1, again, eating out of my palm. Me sensing home, just needing to keep his eyes from meeting my own red-streaked glance.

"I'm in waste management."

Har...

I had held my breath through nearly the whole, beer-soaked piss. The logic being that if I can't smell it, neither can they. It used to work with mom, and it did again. I made the train, and skipped the backseat ride to Folsom. But that was yesterday, or at least very early today, I think. And I'm over it.

So, eventually, the train rolls down the mountain, and, really, I realize, it's no great miracle. Shit can do it, so Amtrak can too. John Hurt sings of a 'hot time in the old town tonight,' and I'm right there with him. Yes indeed. Absolutely. My heart beginning those tired old palpitations again, my underarms moistening with expectation like a virgin, but the kind just saving herself for the right time – prom night, Valentine's Day, that first Friday where mom and dad are out of town and it's not her period. That feeling that It's All Happening, with water somehow on my left out the window now. The trees getting left behind, no doubt to continue to take the battering punishment of all those clouds and all that whiteness. Just standing there, playing their part, doing what they know, swaying. The snow, still coming down, swirling around in those inhuman altitudes, and I'll be down in the city, with lights and barrrom suds and cabs and maple, oak, cherry, whatever to lay my bony elbows on and feel old, tired, grown-up somehow. With a hotel room around the block I can't really afford, and phone calls that should absolutely be made, put-off. With the distance between God and I growing, more so with every hoppy sip. Even though, or maybe because, I saw, saw what he did and what he does up in those mountains. And, me with my red cheeks growing brighter in the warm barroom night, away from it all, and Seattle just ahead, and a hot time in the old town tonight.

12

To say that everyone, at least anyone with a tinkle of wander-lust, with a tinge of America-love, should at some point take a long-distance train ride – to arrive in an entirely new place, maybe even a new climate, weary, dusting coat-shoulders free of road-grime, feeling the fatigue and the hunger and all the miles and having *earned* it – is, well, clichéd. Right now, it even feels like a cliché, as I sling my sack across my back in Seattle's King Station, worn down, sick of the mountains and their never-ending attempt to outdo one another, standing on tip-toes, their severe ridges like the held-high chin of a Russian beauty tennis player-slash-model, or vice versa, on the street, assured in her sweeping unattainability. And all the people, *train people, Oiy!* And the burden of life sud-denly focused within that single strap bearing down on my poor left shoulder, wanting a beer, but wanting to know why I didn't just fly.

And I need to piss, and the Women's is always right in front of me and the Men's always around the corner, and I certainly don't feel like paying for a cab; but there's something nudging me about the whole experience, like a bee in summer you just can't convince as to the unattractiveness of your iced tea. *This was not fun. This crink in my neck was not romantic. Theroux was some kind of fucking wack-a-doo. Get out of here already.* But the train songs are adding up, and under the stomach gurgles, no-sleep irritation, and a new heaviness to the old rucksack, there is some realization about the al-lure of my directionless journey. Alongside this (down there, in my gut, somewhere around the thankfully stowed-away Mission bur-rito) is a kind of newfound grasp on a fleeting idea just taking root (certainly more solid than the Mission-refried bean shit also growing) – a never before understood sanctity of the whole big shebang surrounding the notion of a 'day off.' Why had I not done this before? I asked it even before I left, while my finger danced hesitantly over Amtrak's 'Book It' button back home, something frightening about the newness coming so late in life. Yes, why not: Waste one of my 10 precious days a year; schlep a week's supplies around a utilitarian station where there's always a Wet Floor sign and somebody mopping and the bathroom still smells like shit; mope about buildings more depressing even than that one terminal at Milwaukee's General Mitchell Airport that somehow exists without a bar; sip stale coffee and eat industrial-strength-microwaved hot dogs on dirty blue cloth seats; merely gaze out the window; to never be comfortable and for the never-comfort to be long-lasting, chronic. Willfully chronic. Surrounded by so many train people and conductors with funny hats. Instead, you stupid moron, yes you with the boxers that need to be changed, the semi-permanent kink in your neck, and probably at least one brand of cold or flu, you could just *get* there. Orbitz, a cab to the airport, *done.*

But this time the need to be there was even less pressing than the need to be back. This stew, a gumbo of time and priorities and responsibilities, this slush and mush of days, now somehow achieved, was the whole point.

So, 22 hours and some 1,000-plus-miles later, countless snow-nipped peaks and not enough leg room, and where was I? Barely arrived at the old platitude about journeys and destinations? A cliché I can now just barely even plaster together in my sleep-deprived, train station-annoyed mind. To think how far I am from a drink and from my manicured itinerary – that one token of organized adulthood in a sea of waywardness, still back in a sad North Beach waste basket – is almost too much to bear on top of this tired truism I just rode through the night to see.

You can do better than this, right, student of profound journalism?

Mr. Scribe of the Night? Celine of Modern America, eh? That's really your final arrival, Mr. Careful Pen-Toting Observer?

...

I exit the station, so like every other station, into the dreary Seattle night. And like nobody's ever seen it before, like it's never been put to paper, yes, it is raining, in Seattle.

Nobody had quite told me about the hills in Seattle. And I'm sure nobody had told them about me. Or my boots. And cliché or not, about the stomping havoc we were about to reign down upon this cloudy old Pacific outpost. There was an impression, in my head, certainly, of the sea and the distant ferry and the grayness, big forearms hefting impossibly heavy pint glasses to knit-hatted, gray-bearded heads in dingy bars, fish flying, and Hendrix's first few notes on *Band of Gypsys* accompanying every image. But it was also as if all the hills of old Frisco had found me, followed me maybe, determined to play the stage props to my little role of errant sailor on West Coast shore leave.

And play it they do. From tattooed lesbian bartenders in a 24-hour diner near the Space Needle, telling me with a smile that I look tired; to the bald-headed bottle-tilter of the Zig-Zag café, who pours me another and offers a "this one's on me," with a more gracious nod than I could ever repay or cover in tip, though I try. From Belltown, to the not-quite-late-night-enough classy holes around Pike's Place, I don't drink beer as much as I drink hops: pure, unadulterated Cascade hops, actually, so much less show-offy, so much more useful than those grossly high ridges from where they take their name.

And strikingly, disarmingly, between those bars and my $4 tokens toward physic happiness and psychological comfort, sit The Homeles: laying, spooning, sprawling *everywhere*. In bands one has to wonder as to the root of. Reminding me of something. Something waiting? Signifying something and nothing of my own vagabond sojourn. Signifying even less and even more as I head to the hopping drag of Pioneer square, cell phone to ear, verifying the deposit of my well-deserved severance paycheck. And I notice how some here frighten, like the familiar Milwaukee bums, eerily tall, something crack-pipe cantankerous and foreboding. But more, most here actually, look better, a Manifest Destiny-resignation across crackly thin skin, content, ready to die. And how peaceful I think – a bottle of Tokay between the legs, the mountains in sight, a wet ocean breeze to smack you off to nevermore. Violent, maybe, as the wind and the weather is in these parts. But certainly less so than the snap of the rope and a broken neck.

I figure these old hoboes have it right, maybe even a few strained notes from out the doors of the Highway 99 Blues Club, making their way through the mist, under the overpass, to accompany a final act. And so it is my idea, I decide. My vision. Much more original than a slack of yellow nylon rope, and a back porch in some California town. So unoriginal, so cliché. Nobody's going to read that.

And I see it, all the way home, through the drizzle on a sad last night in a new city, the rain by now so ubiquitous I've grown accustomed, as have my vices, my crutches: I'm even remembering how to smoke, the Camel between thumb and forefinger, the other fingers playing their part as an umbrella, a shield. Just keep the fire burning, no matter what you do. And my little plumes join the immensity of the Pacific Ocean humidity. And I'm feeling tomorrow's hangover already coming on – airport hangovers, somehow, always the worst – and chowing a burger with furious last meal passion, dripping bacon and gouda grease over the sheets and pulled-back comforter, in only my boxers and pitted-out t-shirt, not even caring about the stank rising from my blistered feet. Taking a shower before bed, just for the one last perk of leaving my towel on the foor. Rising in the morning, to blearily bid adieu to my loving, expensive little space. And how it breaks my heart: To pass this transition with a hotel room, every time – once new, an enticing, fresh destination of crisp, professionally-applied sheets and no nightmares, then it's 'home' for a while, with my socks on the floor and a towel tossed over the door, with my current read on the back of the toilet, a hangover glass of water on the nightstand, the restful sanctuary from elements and too many beers and the menacing smoke-bummers of Belltown, and for then it only to expire, out of my life forever, within a matter of too-few hours that at the end you'd give anything to get back. And then to stumble to the cab, and feel the finality in each step, the sadness of every splash tinking down on the sidewalk. To plop, so beleaguered, so gloomy, so not-refreshed, lowered by my own around-the-clock strive for renewal, new bars, grub, something else at the end of the night. And the cabbie never knowing, never even asking, just going about his day: the right Achilles extends, retracts, hand over hand, a blinker here, a non-blind-spot-check there, and it's really that every destination is just another man's hometown. And plopping the sack down next to me, wishing I could put a sticker on it like they used to do, in black-and-white movies where you can still smoke in the airport, wishing it was one of those old brown cases, now with 'Seattle' prominent and proclamatory, a flag in the snow of some mountain, I'm gazing up and out, and with one last dramatic sweeping survey through the window, lay my head back and say, "airport, please."

Part 2

13

Through the clouds, through the impossibly-paned windows of a Boeing 7-something-or-other, 30-some-odd-thousand feet under the once-white, last clean t-shirt, the grayness of Chicago opens up again below me. Like a man returning home from an orgy – pants a-wrinkle, eyes streaked with red fatal highways, the sun like an out of place bookmark between night and day – the time is ripe for an increase in seriousness.

And so it will be. Or so I tell myself. Or so I told myself before this whole sojourn began. Back when the destination and miles and bars seemed out of reach, infinite, so far away that anything that might come after was unimaginable. When the notion of 'once I get back' seemed such a 50-50 proposition that ideas like 'finding a job,' 'figuring it out,' 'getting my life together,' 'contributing to society' and such, seemed a safe enough distance away to actually be said aloud.

You know, you'll need to find a way to make money.

I'll take care of it.

When?

When I get Back.

No need to support such claims, no accountability necessary at that early juncture.

As soon as I get back will I begin a strict regimen of sit-ups, chin-ups, cardiovascular, no smoking, no drinking, no carbohydrates, no cheesesteaks, more cardio, no more 5am nights, more fiber, less caffeine, some vegetables, almost no burgers, less chicken wings, no more, no more...

And yet, here I am. Descending through the gray gristle of Chicago night air. And these things, these ugly, wretched things – soon to embody my waking existence – once as far away as Monday morning with a 12-pack in the fridge in Friday's happiest hours, will come to pass like the awful asshole buzz of my sworn enemy, the alarm clock.

But awful things never look as bad through the filter of decompression (pizza and a movie on a post-weekend-debauchery Sunday evening, a beer on the walk home from a good show) which is precisely, obviously what a blistered-foot, wearied-liver traveler needs. And upon arrival at O'Hare (whose traffic patterns have become so familiar to me, whose insistence on landing the planes in such rapid-fire succession so obvious, that upon approach I am always leaning forward, awaiting the any-second-now rear ending by the one behind us), there will be a layoff at the parents' sprawling suburban domicile. Halfway between Chicago and Milwaukee. A brief row before the ship of fools is righted once and, maybe, for all. The dividing line between the south of my waywardness, and the north of maturation.

There will be dust blown from my day-planner; itineraries will be less littered with bars and Mexican restaurants and more with appointments and interviews; inventory will be taken; stock, of a spiritual sort, will be analyzed; life will be assessed, refreshed, started anew. My resume will be polished (fuck you, Word, I will figure out that bullet pointing). Cover letters will be sparkled (ah hum, dear reader, what is the proper opening greeting for a cover letter, again? 'Dear Sir or Madam'? Seems so formal...). The cigarettes of my errant ways will be snubbed out, the windows of fresh air smashed open. Doors of my insular ambling will be kicked and tumbled by a wash of networking, striving, and all-around professionalism. Yes, these tasks will initially be performed mostly in nothing but boxers, yes, my grandmother will be phoned for a funds-depleted cushion-check, and yes my severance is still far from worn. So, some leeway. But a die will be cast, one of up-before-noon gravity and clean-nosed seriousness. Laundry will be done, ties will be worn, shoes buffed, and there will be fresh-shaven sobriety.

But this being Chicago, first, there will be pizza.

And not the bullshit, tourist-consumed quiches of sauce and cheese oft-associated with my closest southern neighbor of a city. But the quarter-inch-thick, crisped doughy bed of spiced red gravy, mozzarella and pepperoni.

So, once my big bird touches down (turning so quickly, as if I don't notice, ah hum, Mr. Air-Traffic Controller, so as to not get ass-fucked by the next Boeing schnoz literally sniffing behind us), once the checked bag is shoulder-hoisted, once the cab line is negotiated, the call is placed from the backseat at 85 mph's on I-94. And 35 miles to the north, my greeting mat is being laid: spooned tomato-y gobs over that warm, welcoming dough.

Less than an hour and more than 50 bucks later, my boots are off for what feels like the first time in weeks. I air my scabbed Achilles, and quietly cursing Seattle's 45-degree Capitol Hill, crack a bottle of red, obviously expensive, wine lying on the kitchen island. Around me the surroundings of my pre-adult home are near impossible to digest after a 2-week plight of boxcar blinds, beans, and nights under the overpass. Everything is immaculate, plush, warm, overstuffed. Cats – friendly, nourished – everywhere I turn. Couches with fleece-like blankets over their backs, near impossible to rise out of. And so I find myself comfortably stuck at the moment, reclined at just the right angle so my wine glass, stem between fore-finger and thumb, can rest plum on my empty, gurgling gut. My right palm resting gently over the remote on the black leather next to me. Feet on the coffee table. The 50-some-incher warming and aglow. I could fall asleep, the miles and dust behind me; or I could get drunk, shitty drunk, and let the party go on. Or I could not move. Yes, definitely, I could not move.

I think of calling out to my mother, infantile, yes, spoiled, maybe, but her so happy to see her weary rambler, and who am

I to curb such maternal excitement? Ask her to bring me a fresh T and maybe some slippers. But of course, in my euphoric pre-pizza, wine-drinking contentment, I had forgotten for a moment that my parents are, perfectly, in Mexico. That above-modest playground of the middle-aged and gainfully employed. While here, their drifter world-weary son has yet to leave the country, and at the moment could not even *think* about moving from this very spot.

Not for anything.

It is just the kind of emptiness and silence I used to yearn to fill. Weeks ahead I would scheme: ok, their going to be in the city all night, Ry will score the booze, Bean's got some dope, everyone will park around the corner, I've got all my Stones CD's... Now, liquor so familiar, pot so second hand, the excited sense of a party so tired, my biggest vice is whatever combination of cheese, meat, bread and fryer is closest to hand. The most sensual allure: that fuzzy blanket draping the couch. The ultimate boner of the mind: sitting.

But there's the bell and there's my pizza. And I'm running. Before I know it, moving at an extraordinary rate through the echoey house and a shooing gaggle of startled cats. 20 clasped firmly in hand, I swing the huge front door around to reveal my pie, my eyes honing immediately, but, more striking, astonishing, wielding the said joy-bringer is Patrick Ewing himself. Yes, cue Marv Albert.

As is so often the case with former high school acquaintances at a glance, I remember the nick and not the real name. But the high cheek bones, big always-glistening forehead and long, perpetually dumb-looking face immediately take me back to the playground, and to the flying elbows, surprising agility, oafish intensity and garbage low-post moves of the man currently holding my pizza. Here is Patrick Ewing.

"Ski!?" Surprise. Question. My travel-dom stranger-ness instantaneously and finally shattered.

"Ewing!" Fact.

An awkward man-hug ensues as well as possible with the X-large pie, cardboard of mozz sticks atop, between us. A sort of straight-armed grasp of one another's shoulders. Me, with my right hand underneath, always supporting, always one sure hook under the pizza.

"Thought I was delivering to your parents. You living at home again?" Ewing, nodding, happy, confused.

"Uh, yeah. No. Not, exactly. Just passing through." Me, laughing easy, despite a surprise butterfly of unexpected social anxiety. Silence. Sizing each other up – literally – each thinking, 'damn, he's put on weight.' Each taking stock of the other ubiquitous phenomenon among 'haven't seen you since graduation' pals: the surprising addition of hair to a familiar face. I can feel him eying my patchy sideburns, as I marvel again at the fact that anyone would consciously grow a goatee. A goatee: the bad solo project of a real man's beard.

"Guess you heard about what happened?"

"Yeah." Me, with a strange, almost proud realization of personal loss becoming something of a current event, local gossip, my role therein like a supporting part in a faraway life, at least seen from here, a distant life of substance and occurrences and narratives that I was supposed to be leading.

"You boys were still pretty tight?

"I was with him, right before. In New Orleans."

"Shit, man. What *happened*?"

"We had a blast..."

I flash on drunken smiles in dark bars at 3am around the French Quarter. I flash on dangling feet, craving the dirt, just inches above the ground.

"Yeah, so uhh, we're getting a barrel later down at the 'zebo, if you're not doing anything."

"Shit! You still hang out *there*." I can't keep the surprise out of my voice. Maybe college-asshole, Mr. I'm-gonna-write-a-big-book, came roaring back with one simple exclamation, but I can barely contain myself. As I realize all the years between of errantly discarded joints, cigs, drunken hoots, an occasional fight, not less than a few lines, and police calls haven't rendered the Gazebo – a 10 foot diameter wooden structure on the neighborhood pond, somewhat between houses enough to be comfortable as a high school mecca of bongs and brews – a charred heap, or a condemned zone.

"Yeah. Sometimes." Abashed, Ewing hangs his head. (Marv Albert: "And Ewing is *hurt*!")

"Shit, man! I'll be down." Me, not knowing what else to say.

"Yeah?" Brightening, grinning up at me like he used to after we'd just run a pick-n-roll for the umpteenth time, to close out some local Waukegan hoods in a 2-on-2 at the Township Center. And me, brightening too, flashing on Uncle John's gift and hoping it was still safe in my checked bag.

"Shit, man, I'll bring the *weed*."

On the way back to the kitchen, plopping my 18-incher on the granite-topped island, I take closer stock of the things around me. Stuff, items, merchandise once taken for granted, now, appearing as they might in a Sharper Image catalog of life. Most is not even unattainable, but bafflingly unthinkable. A parallel to flashing on my favorite Brooklyn pies when I'm in my dingy pad, warming up a Tombstone. Stainless steel this, marble that. Hardwood. And the sparkle. And the smell. Pictures in actual frames. And then there is the ultimate sign of comfort and success: a garbage disposal. Where does that garbage go? What class of people have to deal with it and at what point? Shit runs down hill, but what if shit is just, shit!, disposed of. Gone. Evaporated? Right there. Flip of the switch.

I ponder as I chew, sitting at the table, gazing around the kitchen. Doing indescribable – in some places, like in public, illegal – things to the greasy pizza squares in front of me.

Satiated, and post post-orgasm smoke on the big wooden deck under the gray skies, I finally make my way up the stairs for a fresh t-shirt. In my old bedroom, yellowed curling newspaper clippings on the wall, desk and dresser bare, like always the compulsion needs to be filled: through my high school yearbooks I wander. Fingers over faces, tears at the corners of my eyes in spots, a laugh, a headshake. There is my ex-girlfriend, her pre-lost-virginity captured in bright-eyed pre-prom innocence. Back then, her still believing in me. And then there is Kate. Kate is dead. "Kate is dead" I say aloud to myself, as if to make it more real. As if to make it sink in, after what, how long? 8 years? A cat looks up at me from the floor, thinking me crazy, probably.

You don't even know what death is.

Do you, cat?

Don't you see me staring sometimes, just looking into thin air?

I always wondered about that...

(wide-eyed, looking over my shoulder)...

So...?

Man, you don't wanna know...

Certain pages I skip over, not ready. Certain signatures in the back flap I avoid. Now, there is Liz, almost done with med school these days, podiatry, I hear. What is podiatry? Isn't that what the Greeks used to be in to? And there is Ann, living in, what is it, Switzerland? And there is Ewing, again, here smooth-faced, brighter eyes, less defeated, less disappointed, but the same expression. Like play dough, the sparkle in the orbs so different than the future doctors and lawyers and mothers and businessman's wives and martyrs around him, not promising things greater than a couple of really good, well-timed jokes out at the bar on Friday night. And maybe that's enough, for some, for him, for me. This face I used to be able to read like a book, used to just *know*, instinctively, instantly, unthinkingly when it and the lanky body underneath were going to cut to the basket. Pass, *Now*! I think about him currently, think about joining him down at the 'zebo. Burning one, patting each other's beer guts and "member when?"-ing, staring at the pond, me miming jump shots over him, randomly turning and sticking my ass into his midsection, backing him up with a shouting command of "Box out, Box out!," warm Miller Lite out of a can. Comfort in numbers. And the number of cans is very high. Just like the old days... *'Member when?*

But instead, fresh-socked and clean-shirted, I find myself drifting back to the couch. Hulling the pizza box to the coffee table, now for round 2.

Tomorrow the alarm will ring, no matter how many times I hit snooze. Even if I unplug the fucker, rip the cord out and Joe Pesci the bitch into little fragments. Stomp it good, and keep the curtains closed, the cats locked out, bury my head in a heaping mess of billowing blankets. It will be ringing. For tomorrow, I'll be back, home, tomorrow I will take care of things. But mostly, if I try, it's at arm's length; and I ease back on the black leather, let it envelope me, reach for the pizza box, nestle it atop my beer bulge, flip to HBO. Nearly 10 HBO's and movie channels I haven't even heard of. I can't remember what it's like to have cable, and the house is dark and loud with silence around me. And there will be ringing, and there will be shit to be seen to. I pull the cover up further, around my chin, a fleece-type thing undoubtedly from Alpaka or some fucking animal I couldn't even describe, and it has less to do with my failures as a writer and more to do with thick-skulled ignorance. But I wrap myself in warmth and insouciance as rain tinks the windows on a cold Chicago March night. And tomorrow is far enough away.

14

But really, please, somebody, how exactly does one go about writing a novel? Just looking for that spark, the impetus. The opening line. A *zinger*. Really it's all I need, and the rest will take care of itself, come rolling out like so much Saturday morning diarrhea. I can hear myself explaining it to curious Rolling Stone or maybe Esquire writers, maybe a year, maybe a few years from now… *'Ya know, I'm not really sure where it came from', says Ski, lighting a smoke and adjusting his shades as the waitress at our sunny West Village café pours him another Johnnie Gold. 'I just tried not to think about it'*… Is that actually a good opening line, right there? No. It should be something I overheard on the bus. Or something. It certainly shouldn't start with the word 'The' - this is about all I can ascertain from the creative impulse, at the moment. So the screen stares back, blank. I'm leaning toward 'If,' have already typed and deleted it a number of times actually, just to get the finger-blood flowing. Something about the ring of it, something about the range of possibilities it leaves open. *'If* only he could get off his ass…' *'If* only he could find that opening line.' Propositional. That's some shit!

And so I sit in front of my parents' computer, trying not to think about it. Milwaukee, yes, is as far away as it was 2 days ago, when I sat in just the next room and fantasized on the mounds of applications and progress that would be under my ass by this advanced point. When I thought the hours would begin to fly like they do in movie montages of people doing hard work, or getting shit together with focus, teamwork, Rocky-training-type stuff. When things would be scribbled off, in pen, maybe even a sharpie, from the dayplanner. Good, consecutive sober nights of sleep, vegetables, vitamins and the sights set on tomorrow. But at the moment the best gauge of time and the passage of days seems to be the diminishing quantity of leftover pizza squares currently sitting in the refrigerator. This is something I definitely try not to think about.

If only he had more pizza...

The kitchen island is littered with empty wine bottles, the corks currently the object of a high-stakes game of kittie World Cup. It's been engaging for all of us, to say the least, as the black one – obviously the favorite, what with the heft and height advantage – has been yet unable to truly capitalize over the scrappiness of the pudgy gray thing that never says die. I've lost a bit of shut-eye, certainly, as the two and sometimes the third feline violently trounce each other over the vast hardwood playing field till all hours of the night. But I can't bring myself to stop their game. Such is the passion! My eyes haven't been as wide as theirs are now – ever. Nor could I bring myself to look away, just last night, while sitting at the kitchen table, Uncle John-joint between thumb and forefinger, ash tray and Cabernet in front of me, as the gray one Pele-ed and stampeded endlessly across the floor, and in one overly-heroic jaunt, unable to apply the brakes in time, failed to stop her poor head from cracking into the base of the refrigerator. But only, undaunted, unfazed, she turned and tore ass in the other direction, after the cork, which had somehow – cat physics! – bounced back the other way in the process. And so the dance continued: the black one yielding, the gray one pursuing, my glass practically refilling itself as the glaze grew thicker over the eyes.

But, in between such moments and the pizza, at least some serious movement has been made: New strings, finally, have been placed on the Epiphone, retrieved from the hardcase in the high school bedroom. And throughout this solo 48-hour tour, there has been a ceaseless waterflow of mind-storming. A major work of high seriousness feels, inevitably, just around the corner. So I strum and pick, HBO dancing in LCD before me, breaking every 45 minutes or so for a fresh cup of coffee (during the dreaded daytime hours, that is), and a new turn on the office chair facing down Microsoft Word. I've taken to walking around in a cape – a satiny edged fleece blanket from my high school bed, draped over the shoulders just so. And like this I wander: Kitchen, living room, office, back to the kitchen to retrieve the coffee, a shit in the downstairs bathroom, a trip upstairs before I forget my coffee, head back downstairs, look for it, find it on the kitchen island, cold now (too long of a shit), so I make more, close the edge of the blanket around my torso and head back to the couch, pick up the guitar, wait for the brewing.

2 days so far, and I figure another 2 could put me on track. Definitely, by the end of not this, but next weekend, I'll be up and out of the safety net. Alright, April, May, absolute latest.

A glance at my greasy hair or crusted boxers, as well as my ignorance of the relative temp outside or precise day of the week, leaves no doubt that the one-time jealousy over my rootless Western wandering would be long gone if any of the old gang could see me now. But after the bars and miles, there's also something newly monkish, ascetic about this existence. Invisible Man, I'm thinking, or that sore-livered character out of Dostoyevsky. Just waiting on the spark, the start. I've withstood my damage; now the righteous flow of fuck-you genius just needs to be tapped, unleashed. Furious wisdom will spew, oh how it will spew. Just waiting on that first line. And then.

The discipline, at least, has been there though. Enough even to ignore all three of Ewing's calls – his name on the caller ID, like so many of the high school-pal variety, so foreign and out of place looking. On the other hand, 'Mom Cell,' popping up in the digital light blue, is oh-so familiar, and eventually, every now and then, is to be taken.

"How's the weather?" Me, answering, avoiding the unavoidable for a couple minutes.

"Unbelievable, 80 everyday..." Her, taking the bait, but kind of rubbing my nose in it at the same time.

Yeah, how was Seattle in March, dumbass?

"I got home safe." Me, accentuating the positive of recent achievements...

"That's great honey."

"The cats are great." Me, again, now, throwing the focus to others, but I'm keeping them alive, and so, you see, my victories here are mounting.

"So..."

And here it comes.

"The gray one is actually winning..." Me, desperate...

"What have you been *doing*?"

And the implication and emphasis on 'doing' is plenty to pierce the soul and all hard-won contentment.

"Well, I started working..."

"Yeah!?"

"On growing a beard"...

"..."

"I've fed the cats." Again, not sure why she's failing to offer affirmation.

"Ted, this is serious."

If only he hadn't answered the phone...

"You're not going to believe who I saw." Me, searching.

"..."

"Ewing!" Forced excitement lighting up his name.

"Yeah. Figured. He still delivers our pizzas."

The emphasis on 'still' and the general flatness of the statement causing such a wave of pity for the goateed post-player that I vow to call him back as soon as I hang up.

"Maybe he can get you a job?"

"Yeah, I asked him..."

"And."

"It's kind of a union thing."

"Delivering pizzas is a union thing?"

"Yeah. You don't know how these teamsters are."

I flash on purple-veined, ripped, salt-and-pepper haired forearms, heaving and hoing, tossing and laughing, deep, barrel-chested voices coming out of brown uniforms. The blue-collar camaraderie rap that used to bookend all my weekdays. I flash on the continuation, sans me, the world spinning, those muscles still extending, flexing, pulling. Action everywhere, all around my blanket-caped ass.

If only he hadn't been born with a silver spoon....

"Well as long as you're gonna be at home..."

"No." Me, interrupting, with what feels like the first forceful thing I've said in months.

"They'd love to see you"...

"I'm not ready."

"Jeez, when he was alive"…

"Yer breaking up, I'm going through a tunnel."

"You practically lived at their house…"

"I'm hanging up."

"It's just right down the street…"

And with that something breaks and something else falls away. Only half-listening to mom's rest-of-the week itinerary of massages, shrimp in poblano sauce on the beach, catamarans (what the fuck is a catamaran?), I begin furiously finger-banging the computer mouse back and forth, willing the cursed machine awake. Ready somehow. The diarrhea gates are slowly opening. Veins on my hands are popping and the fingers are going themselves. I'm hanging up on mom (parting words: "don't drink the water or buy drugs on the beach").

Themes of regret, metaphors, clichés, oh the clichés!, are playing bumper car in my mind. I'm dialing Ewing, suddenly eager to see him later. "Zebo, beers," I'm yelling at his voicemail. Words are coming out. I'm smiling at a cat standing in the doorway. Then my furrow-browed gaze is back on the screen. Sun is blinking through my cape. Words are going down.

    '*If* only he had never walked down that street.'

15

So, how I end up heading South, rather than North and home, is, well, difficult and maybe even embarrassing to explain. What I'd like to do, as I'm sitting here – again, ass-palmed by a blue polyester Amtrak seat, training backwards this time, 16-oz. Caribou in hand, barreling toward the big city – is chalk up the brief parlay to great progresses made. Five pages written though, double-spaced, over 3 full days, probably hardly qualifies. What I'd also like to do is remain steadfast in denial about any notion that I just may be running away from the inevitable cavalcade of responsibilities waiting just across the Wisconsin border. From unpacking on down the mere thought of Milwaukee flat wears me out. But, 'lazy man' aside, this can't be it. Neither is it the return home by my parents, tomorrow, with their endless questions and fresh sunburns, a true motivator for the last second flight response. Though this may seem suspect.

Really, honestly, mostly it has to do with phalluses. Black ones. And that feel down near my gut (butterflies? Last night's chorizo? Love?), that comes crawling back every time that skyline opens up, revealing itself like the greatest of teases: side-cleavage there, and the train rounds a slight turn and its outta sight, a whole lotta leg there, but now only visible out the other side's window, and I'm craning my neck and salivating. Eventually, the loin-tingle well underway, two perfect, misshapen, endless rods of man and all his possibility sit in plain view, puncturing the quivering helpless blue sky. Dark, hulking steel. Is it wrong to be aroused? Try to think of them in more hetero terms I might: the endless calves of the Sears, spiky nips atop the Hancock. Ebony seductresses. But it seems a stretch, and what's the point? My lips are drooling and I can practically taste beef on my tongue, wafting up from the distant stockyards.

The train winds by the always-gridlocked traffic and we're already passing Peterson, Irving Park, and the slot machine game is going hard through my window: backs of brownstones, rickety wood balconies, then breaking onto major streets and tiny little plazas and their breathtaking pizza joints. Then more butts-of-apartments. Garbage bags and charcoal grills on wooden decks and butts-of-lives. Fascinating like a plumber kneeling under the drain, hard to look away. Little speed-of-train glimpses into the annals of big-shoulder existence. I breathe deep the recycled Amtrak air, try to recall more such Chicago clichés. There's someone from the Rat Pack going in the recesses of my mind, but whichever one quickly gets pushed out by the pleading twang of Robert Johnson. *C'monnn...* How could that baby not want to go?

Together, we've had a weird sort of relationship, Chicago and I.

Once, there was a friend of mine, a roommate actually, and a guitar-playing sort of college buddy with a near-perfect penchant for proper rock and blues but a completely insufferable proclivity to really overbelt the vocals on Saturday nights. Greenwich Village-Dylan style. *Easy, easy* I would say. But he thought I was ribbing. So on he would go, drowning out my tasty solo runs, piercing eardrums, eyes-closed in concentration and head back, thinking himself rather cute. Soulful, even. The ladies ate it up, as college ladies will do. At one time, a friend of his, stoner sort of high school buddy all the way from Oregon or some such place had come to town for one of those random, ridiculous college weekends. Only he came on neither soulful nor cute – as associations with the assailing songster might point to. In fact, he didn't come on at all, this one. This friend of a friend. He simply sat back on our couch, 'yeah, yeah,' leaning forward when engaged, nodding, in his baseball cap and khakis, no pretense, talking about jazz, just wanting a couple thankful beers and a place to crash, rapping about albums, packing nice herb, smiling, bleary-eyed, all the way from out West, with *thoughts* on Kind of Blue and not just the poster on his wall, agreeing, bonding, *listening...* "Whaddayou think?"

A couple of crazed smoky nights was all it took for consummation, and we kept in touch through the years. Always right there, but never quite mine. He offered a pleasant surprise every couple weeks in the email inbox. But still, remained just out of reach. Ungraspable. Only friends through association. Me, craving more of the familiarities and less of the conversational niceties; jealous and annoyed with the knowledge that my new friend was keeping better touch with the 'Tangled Up in Blue'- shouting asshole.

But maybe it was just because there were only a couple of those mad, high nights. This friend-of-a-friend and I, we never argued about whose turn it was to take out the trash, who pissed on the seat, who ate the last piece of pizza. And so it goes with Chicago. The Hancock whets my appetite, the Sears renders blood to the tip, Robert Johnson sings, moans about it and I weep, covertly, like an immigrant every time that skyline casually, sexily – *I knew you'd want s'more big daddy* – asserts itself in the big glass train window; and the pains of Loop-parking and Daly-leadership and rents and urban sprawl will never interfere with our happy little back door affair.

He – or she, if that makes you more comfortable – keeps me coming back, wanting more, more familiarity, more knowing glances, more people asking me for directions to Al's and not the other way around; more old-friend laughs.

Even though, indeed, I was on pace, on target, on task just last night before the self-congratulatory walk down to the 'zebo...

"Hey man, so what happened with the job?"

"Fired."

"No, shit?"

"Yeah. Caught having sex with my secretary."

"What kind of shipper/receiver has a secretary?"

"A top-shelf shipper, and, uh, receiver."

"Shit. Was he hot?"

Har-Har.

And so it always goes. Shooting the shit, as they say. And shoot it we did, Ewing and I. Gliding back into the easy chair of teenage-acquaintanceship. Once he had established I hadn't become the big-city prick he feared, and once I had established he hadn't completely morphed into the kind of bitter, alcoholic, backwoods, townie-Deliverance-type fuck driving the same car from high school, smoking endless cigarettes in a gross, depressing way, working retail or as a bar back, the living in the basement type that always kept me checking the rear view mirror of my mom's ride while driving those scary suburban streets.

"You know what, it's so easy." Me taking a long toke, noticing he'd become quite professional at joint-rolling since senior year.

"Yeah?" His eyes twinkling, like somebody had just offered making a two-on-two matchup a bit more interesting…

"I write a book. I get it in a library. I go on tour."

"Just like that?"

"Who's stopping me?"

"Not me."

"You?" Me, sticking an accusatory, challenging index finger into at his chest.

"Not me, man."

"You? Ducks!?" Me, suddenly springing to life, ready to charge the quacking, floating, scheming bastards sidling toward the pond shore at the foot of the 'zebo. Emboldened by Ewing's encouraging laughter, feeling sprightly, stupid the way high school drunks could be. And of course, anger at the offending duck family. In the 18, 19, 20-year days, something would have been unleashed at this point, uncorked, to some end: hurled empty bottles, a roar and heedless sprint toward the water's edge, an expletive-laced tirade against Donald Duck at the top of lungs, something hideous and immature and worthy to be filed in the 'Member' When?' category. But, along the way, at the point where I lost count of the score, was busy fiddling with the this is this and that is that, liquor had dropped the ability to make me feel that young. And last night, eyes glistening, I had remained upright, mostly, serene, something like an adult. In control, seemingly, at least from the outside. I let it drop and Ewing's laughter had receded, down-shifted, the way laughs do into 'ahh's…

And so I'm here. Rolling into town like Muddy Waters. Not exactly sure what to expect other than something completely different than the cottonfields and moonshine I'm accustomed to. Ready to mix and shake it up. Ready for a deal, a rent party or two. Ready to *plug in*. Maxwell Street. The Brothers Chess. The train barreling and chuggin' on in with a great whistle, me with my last-second ticket, pulling in through the back-door, someone up on high in that great skyline saying "I know you, rider." And me in my dusty derby, Stella axe in hand, bought from Mr. Sears himself, right here, all the way from Memphis, standing-room only on the old M&O. And the wonders of direct deposit, and the impossible miracle of all that severance pay floating through mythic lines of information, right into the good-times wallet of my front cords pocket. Now *that's* what R.J. was moaning about. Relief from the prick of king cotton and the locusts wailing, and baby, yes, I wanna go.

And it's the giddy excitement of seeing a friend, not old but far from new. Not known, but the strange providing something more. Not just more armpit sweat, yes, maybe that too, but something. Just one more, before I get serious. Chicago, right there, such an easy provider of that one more. *One more*, like the bluesmen say, knowing, but not quite knowing for certain, there's a good four more choruses on the way. One more.

16

Generally a certain amount of planning, foresightedness, intuition – maybe not itinerary-length, like some assholes – but something, is to be recommended upon any venture to a big city. When you roll in and the vast glass-and-granite endlessness of downtown stretches every which way of the compass, including, now, in Chicago, Up. Pining for the sky. And down, too. Toward that murky nasty river that snakes around the Loop, collecting the squalid waste of every dream of every hobo wandering; and looking meaner and meaner the colder that Lake Michigan wind blows. As it is now, while I exit Union Station onto Canal. Those peaked skyscrapers, and the funny one cut in half at an angle, like by a giant with a sharp cleaver or obsessed with beveling, all so picturesque, pristine from my train window seat, suddenly swallowing me up, maliciously, like the bypassed Cascades of so long ago. Though it's coming on April, the dreary February-ish aura of everything still sleeping or dead is malingering like the last one at a party.

Dude – yawning – we're, uh, outta beer.

That's cool.

So...

Yeah, I'll just have some water. What was I saying?

Yes, it's best to have direction. Or at least look like you do, before the tear-tattooed and hospital-braceleted panhandlers start their pounce. Telling stories, asking questions, bumming smokes, always with the disarmingly specific amount of money requests ("yo, you got 37 cents?"), eyeing the 'from Wisconsin' bullseye on the back of every shirt I own.

Standing there, over the river, struggling to light a smoke, I think of the drizzly fog in Frisco, the rain in Seattle, now this - whipping air, spewing forth down West Adams like a streaking drunk. Pummeling goosebumped forearms. I vow someplace warm will be next. Someplace chill, as they say – I hear them say that – as opposed to this every-which-way bone-chilling. Shivering, always a body and wardrobe struggle toward comfort, the underarm sweat cooling and doubling in its own unpleasantness. The next one will be the friend that makes me want to stay up all night, after that keg is long kicked. Even when we're both out of cigarettes.

But part of being here so plan-less, hopeless in the gusting air, is actually to be without a plan. Though that's a bit presumptuous, thinking on it like I had any choice. For as soon as I de-train, down those metal steps into that bowel-like tunnel below Chicago, and out into the gray, exiting Amtrak's uniformed, starch-hat orderliness, any plan at all would be utterly futile. And any thoughts of on-the-beach bullshitting, board shorts, hammocks or frilly umbrella-ed drinks would be as ridiculous as suggesting such said niceties to Ditka himself.

The big car pulls up, Oldsmobile of some sort, belying it's relatively new-ish age with a series of bumper crevasses, a plethora of dent/scratches and scratch/dents – none of which look from the same incident. With the back driver's side tire near-flat, front Illinois plate hanging by one rusted screw, my ride spots me and edges in front of a honking taxi toward the curb on Adams. Smiling, reaching for the handle, through the window I can already spy the ubiquitous red and white Marlboro pack resting in the middle console cup holder, and with a glimpse I'm taken back on one thousand pot runs, one hundred drunken rides, and the everyday-after-school unfettered release that the world a friend's car used to entail.

My pickup is a half-hour late, thus, for Bean, about 10 minutes early.

I'm happy to get out of the wind. And Bean is happy to see me. I can tell this because he takes a second to carefully lay his Taco

Bell chalupa on his groin, lick his ring finger of grease and give me a hardy how-ya-doin' slap on the sternum, still chewing (beef, as I can smell), not smiling, nodding, as I'm settling in.

"Dude." Me, smiling, unrumpling sweaty boxers by raising my ass off the seat, then back down, shrugging my shoulders for warmth, settling in.

"Want any hot sauce packets, buddy?" Bean, shifting it back into gear, not checking his blind spot – the other kind of those two kinds of people – chomping into the oozy tortilla again as we pull out.

"Depends on the flavor."

"Fire. For you, man. Fire." Bean, smiling now, his teeth yellowing noticeably for the first time. Me, flashing on high school when the threats of cigs seemed far enough in the future as to be rendered some kind of foreboding science fiction. Suggestions that would need to be heeded by people that we'd never become.

"Where we headed?"

"The end of the night."

"Yeah?"

"But first, I gotta stop and see a guy."

Dean Moriarty, yes, that all 'yeah'-saying hero of every 18-year-old with a library card and a pulse, may have been a parody of a real life man. But he also, just maybe, could have been part-portraiture of this high-school buddy, now slouched before me in all wide-eyed, patchy beard, stained-hoodie glory. Though it's a bit early in the day, the comparison becomes more and more evident later, exponentially, once the light fades. If you catch him at just the right after-midnight, red-eyed hour. Especially if you catch him behind the wheel. But, as more than a few cops scattered over various Midwestern cities could attest to in their more honest moments, not the policeman's ball hearty laughing times of camaraderie, this can be hard to do.

And here I am again drifting, with the meanness of black downtown slouching toward old familiarity. At once both at home and privileged in my ol' rider seat. My direction thrown out the window. Us, sometimes chasing it, sometimes leaving it behind with the acceleration of the purplish, ground beef-scented car.

"How's life in the Program?" Bean, the chalupa gone, now replaced in his lap by a red glass bowl, which he's simultaneously filling with greens while pointing the car north, on Orleans.

"Ain't easy, man. Had to leave everything behind. Looking over my shoulder everyday now."

"I always knew you were a rat bastard stool pigeon fuck."

Aside from such conversational 'eff you' somersaults, our relationship always has been based on movement. Neither of us can remember exactly when consummated – some say an English class, though the on-the-basketball court folklore is the story the two of us tend to favor – but for me it was like riding an empty highway, and it taking someone flying by in the left lane for the realization of how slowly I was going. How placated. How pacified. Zeppelin, weed, Petty, beer, Stones, cigs: suddenly amalgamated into some unspoken credence of euphoria and elevated heartbeats. It was some Gospel of the Gas pedal, and all that possibility of the seemingly endless streets paving the very few miles between our parents' suburban homesteads.

Driving around together, passing a pipe, as we suddenly are now, Chicago streets growing into familiar north side neighborhoods, Halstead becoming Milwaukee, nondescript between-land becoming packed, trendy Wicker Park, it is hard not to recall doing the same over the same said ground before a distant friend's wake.

Years ago: Nostalgia and pot yielding the usual stony sentimentalisms, we cruised the North Side, putting off inevitable arrival. Once we pulled up, eventually, the black surrounding us (me being one of the few I know without a black suit, as if not having one presupposes me from all serious funeral-activity) everyone was doing that somehow inherent, conciliatory smile-nod thing in awkward, restrained greeting. Hugs, etc. Us, then not knowing that this is the way it went, getting out of the car, collectively agreed, "this sucks." Looking at each other and wishing we had smoked less pot, were less paranoid, were dressed nicer, knew we'd best stick together through this thing.

It was the first in an NBA playoff-length series of goodbyes. One after one, with the season's blending into each other, the temperatures changing, and then changing again, and us, at that point already picturing ourselves rather seasoned, grizzled, hip to this being this and that being, well, we had no clue.

Now again we're on the subject, nothing but a bowl and growing comfort between us, me going soft, unperturbed, wistful, taking control and turning up the heat for myself; hardly paranoid with Bean's meathooks steering my person with something more than authority.

"So, you were home, go by Ry's parents?"

"Nah."

"Shit. You were right there."

"Not ready… Or something."

"_"

"I know, I know. I will, I will."

"_"

"You're right, I'm going to."

"_"

"One of these days..."

"_"

"Should I?"

"You should do what the fuck you want, man." And Bean says this quickly, with the strangest mix of flippancy and fuck-to-itiveness. We each take another hit, and the car is rounding itself onto

Irving Park already, Chicago's sprawl and forlorn industrial packets meshing into a view of sudden, barren sadness. And it may be hard to act the drifter, wanderer, hobo, itinerant bluesman when you have a guide. A guide with a big car full of welcoming drugs and fast food essence. But with the gray-ish backdrop of Bean's preferred cruising grounds – the crumbling brick and bus stops, the bro's with their hoods up, the check cashing boxes of buildings with sad neon lights, the general disarray of scattered hot sauce packets and empty cig boxes at my feet, the black-ish smears all over the cheap leather, the filled ash tray, the unshaven hulk accelerating too fast and never signaling and swallowing as much smoke as he exhales – it's easy to feel all those dreamy existences and more.

"Writing much?" Bean, inquisitive, always, pruning me out the corner of his brown eyes. Not happy, but understanding of the situation as a distant uncle might be. Though the questionable state of his own employment status leaves him little in terms of lecture material.

"Yeah, yeah. In fact I gotta meeting with the Chess brothers later."

"Wrong dream, Ski. Wrong dream."

"Ahh…"

With knowing, yellowing smiles, we're lighting smokes, leaning back, the windows cracked and ash and plumes blowing carelessly around the car. Heading back south now, by the Mexican joints and coffee shops of our beloved Boy's Town. Me, telepathically nudging him and the car toward Lake Shore Drive, and Bean picks it up, wordlessly turns left down Barry.

"Got any work lined up, gonna make some money?"

"I'm thinking about maybe starting a pimping business."

"I don't think it works like that."

"No? What is it like a union thing?"

"It's not that. It's that, look at you, you don't have the right shoes."

And we drive, nowhere in particular around Bean's adopted home, and 'member when.' With the condos and Lakeview apartments flying backwards, we marvel, collectively, at the legendary ability of this odd couple to defy all rational decision-making and any nights alone at home. Flashing around and then back again – the tendency ripe when it's been this long between us – we arrive at one of our favorites: It was a night that climaxed with the two of us, stony, on a stranger's couch at 2am on the east side of Milwaukee, being serenaded acapella by a bar-met hippie. "Bridge Over Troubled Water" it was (though Bean mistakenly recalls it as "The Boxer"), with the singer somehow turning devilish, foreboding, a weird Manson-ish glint entering the eye each time his version rose toward the refrain. Bean, sensing the wrong kind of disorder, taking charge as he does, and should, especially with me wafting boozily toward incomprehension and flow with the go and my usual thrust to trust most everyone as the good, non-murdering, not a cult-leader kind of the two kinds of people in the world, and trying to change the subject from the suddenly-nefarious Garfunkel-at-hand, had interrupted with a query as to the whereabouts of the stranger's absent TV.

"I gave it to my friend."

"Yeah? What a guy. Good friend." Bean, placating, peacing, though I can see his fist tensing, can see him taking markedly smaller hits, a sign of needed clarity.

"Yeah, Jesus really needed my TV."

"Oh, your friend, Hey-Zeus?"

"No, his name is Jeez – uuuzz."

That night, just like now, starting with the best of intentions, and a distant notion of going to see a guy.

It was shortly after this TV-less stranger with an over-proclivity toward too-strong marijuana had identified Bean as St. Gabriel ("I know who you are, you're St. Gabriel." "No dude, I'm Beannn."), and around his fiery second verse of "Mr. Tambourine Man," that he paused the rueful wailing and mounting awkwardness to answer a phone in the next room. Glances shooting between us, the tension obvious, even in my zapped farawayness, Bean was suddenly flexing and unflexing a shaking fist toward me as if to say *what did you get me in to?* And *I'm gonna to have to kill this fucking guy, aren't I, Teddy? Aren't I?* And me, shoulders shrugging. Mute with over-doped helplessness. It wasn't until the troubadour returned, ready to continue with the song, informing us now that Jesus – not Hey-Zeus – was, in fact, currently and with great haste, on his way to join the party, that we made a fevered run for it. Tripping over each other like the Stooges on his welcome mat, banging the deadbolt to the left, then properly to the right, not looking back, Bean shoving me ahead of him out the door, feverishly trying to throw his boots on while hopping on one foot then the other in the doorway, yelling "I parked in a tow zone! A tow zone!" But the psuedo Manson was motionless, it somehow scarier that way, and had downshifted to the loud humming of something else. "God Only Knows" we later pegged it, and he sat and grinned in his chair, serene now, awaiting Jesus, probably waiting still, long after Bean and I were bombing down the apartment hallway desperate for an exit and the sanctuary of this same purple-ish car. The both of us giggly, fried, - "woooo," "Jesus!" – survivors.

So here I am again. Settling in, with St. Gabriel driving, and at this we laugh. Har-Har, my stomach tense and sore already from stony over-comedy. But I'm settling in for the ride. Doing what the fuck I want, as Bean might say, lighting a smoke and not caring, the ash settling on my pants. Ready for what might come. Easing back, settling in.

17

Hard to believe the sight of, once it's there in front of your face, and not just some down-the-road notion: the actual image of giving the world hell. In the mirror before me: striped boxers, yellowed white t-shirt, 50's greaser hair (the not-on-purpose kind), the patchy growth of a 17-year-old sprinkled around the growing beer-chin of a man at least thrice that age, crooked glasses hinting toward a slight bent of academia, but the crazy Kaczynski-been-in-the-woods unemployable kind, hand clutching the ever-present coffee cup. Taking it with me now – for comfort, for slurping, for something to appear to be doing with my hands – all around the apartment. So here it is now, again, as I appraise myself and the day's prospects, digging crusts out from the corners of my eyes, contemplating the crack-of-11:30am bowel movement which generally kicks the proceedings off.

I scratch my gut with my left hand, just because that's what it looks like the guy in the mirror would do, violently almost, thinking it might look more natural in an actual wife-beater. Taking a sip of coffee, the wonder creeps as to how bags grow under the eyes despite me batting close to the 12-hours-a-night average (always like the illustrious .400 mark for me). I flush the toilet.

For just like that, I'm home. Exercising some long-neglected pipes and valves. Beginning to neglect the daily need for pants. Or showers. Flushing my *own* toilet, sitting in my *own* chair, and there's little left but the ghosts of noble, hard-won hangovers. The Monday-in-class feel of never having fully appreciated the developing any-direction sprawl of the previous Saturday night. Wistful. Pissed too. For it's all over. To boot is the realization that, amidst the meanderings and still too-quick journey home, I no longer know where my toothbrush is.

Regardless, the solo tour of the lowly recesses of my apartment has begun. Wheels are in motion, the schedule has been cast, dyed, concreted, sharpie-ed, whatever. Backed only by a couple of mostly indifferent cats – *you gonna get up today? 'cuz I'm kinda comforble here on yer feet* – the rigmarole of agenda has begun. And dear god, how it will be begin, completely and whole-heartedly, in earnest, tomorrow, yes, tomorrow, when I will not hit 'snooze', won't even think about it. Certainly not 8 times – at 9 minutes per rip – for a total of 72 bonus minutes of what is, essentially, already bonus sleep. No, the schedule will be maintained. Snooze will be eschewed. Starting tomorrow.

How will it go? Alarm-clock clamoring, coffee percolating, laptop booting, sunshine sunshining, some calisthenics getting the blood flowing. Perkish, optimistic, brow perpetually furrowed. So lost in the search for self – deep in the tangly webs of the internets – as to ignore any growing hunger, empty coffee cup, like Julia Roberts in the Pelican Brief, up all night, head leaning toward the goal, oblivious to the entering Roommate.

And so it goes that, in truth, this has somehow become the highlight of my routine: When I look up from my 4pm bagel break, realize I've had 3, wince that I'm still hungry, note it's already half past five, lower the volume on the ESPN talking heads, or maybe Steven Seagull, and enter into my first non-cat conversation of the day.

"Tough day, buddy?" Roomate, oh how he's enjoying it all, laughing it up, comfortable in the living situation (and thus, pizza ordering situations) since my continual assurances about cushy severance pay and the coming over-stuffed, bean-bag like offerings just around the corner, this time from Uncle Sam.

"I'm on R and R, motherfucker!"

I look forward to it, actually, subconsciously wait on him like a housewife or loyal pug. This one who used to interrupt my writing flow, who impinged any hope of a sexual – solo or otherwise – life, who killed my guitar boners like he was a sleeping Mormon, who consistently brutalized leftover pizza every morning before my asleep-ass had any chance, who's entire definition in my life embodies the inability to live and exist on my own, even while employed. Simply so we can have exchanges like this...

"Hope you don't start getting bed sores, buddy."

"Hope you don't choke on your fucking tie tomorrow, cocksucker."

But, as I ease toward the militarized daily schedule, it's just such waiting that has suddenly become typical. Waiting for an email, a telephone call. Waiting to matter again. Waiting on Unemployment. Waiting on a friend. Waiting for a trip to miraculously plan itself, insert itself into my dayplanner, to just pop up unexpectedly as I'm whiling away and glancing toward the empty whiteness of future weeks. Waiting for something to indicate that I won't need to become a waiter. Waiting to stop writing in Dr. Seuss-speak. Waiting for that line of Kerouac to tell me how to feel again, to open up the summer-possibilities like we were 18 again, when the sun used to feel like the sun and not an indictment on my inactivity, waiting for that magic, energy – instead of this oafish, goon-like unfeeling inconclusiveness.

Yet I read somewhere that standing on a street corner waiting for nobody is power. So, maybe, this is at least halfway toward a proper state of being.

But here, sitting in my bedroom's worn green easy chair, in my boxers, another cup of coffee cooling too fast, another blinking job description on the screen before me far exceeding my ambition, experience (let alone the inertia to apply for it), the blinds perpetually drawn on the ever-intensifying spring, I can't help but feel that tomorrow won't be tomorrow at all. It will be next month. Then August, September. The days bleeding into one another, time at

111

once standing still and running away from me. Undressed days. Wednesday's boxer/t-shirt combo drifting into Saturday's, Sunday's boxer/t-shirt combo.

All the while, former co-workers sit on happy hour patios, libating, laughing.

Anyone talked to ski?

Heard he was dead.

Har-har-har...

Chesty laughs and cigars lit. Tennis rackets resting on the table. White Oxford sweaters tied casually over their necks. Waiters bringing another round of sweating top-shelf Arnold Palmers.

And me, repeatedly clicking 'Inbox', getting it to refresh, and marveling at my TV and how Steven Seagall appears to be the sort that has probably never waited for anything in his life. Conquering shit, kicking ass. Even by himself. Even on a boat. *If you can wait and not be tired by waiting...* That is Kipling's *man*. But here I am, getting it all confused with roundhouse kicks, effortless guitar licks and the ability to successfully pull off that manly man-ponytail.

Torn between the waiting and non-waiting. Waiting 'till I can go back to that street corner, unfettered. Unperturbed. Powerful again, waiting on nobody, except maybe a bus, for my ride, for my places to be. Not waiting for something that, yes, might never come. Not sure either way which is correct, except about the part that at the very least, I need a new toothbrush. Or maybe not.

18

And so it hits me like one of those dreams, where you're falling and you wake with a jerk, and in that instant you realize you are not only safe, but immaculately, in a bed, which would have broken the fall anyway. And you feel a bit foolish for not having known that cushiony mattress was there, all along, and a bit relieved, and much more comfortable than during all that unnecessary falling time.

Should have known that's the way it would go, would have to go: none of that fitful knuckle-ringing, brow-furrowing, worry/planning ever leads anywhere, anyways, anyhow. But rather, it's in those peaceful interludes, those moments between notes, the quiet sudden clarity ringing like something out of Hesse. Siddhartha, I believe, and it must be because that's the only one I ever read. So, similarly, unexpectedly, waking from an exceptionally humid July night in a moist ball of tangled sheets, cats disrupted and gone from my erratic sleep, window air-conditioner gurgling and humming and ineffective, there it is, the soft curves of the only one I have ever loved staring back at me in the low light. Slouching against the dresser in all her pear-shaped lowdownness. Sultry, bottom out and head back, always expectant and seductive, if just a bit rigid outside of my knowing, greasy palms.

Yes, I should have a guitar stand. And yes, she should be back in her case sheltered from the sweaty elements. But had she on this fateful night been tucked away and safe, the realization may have never come. That perfect mix of ale in the veins, green in the brain receptors, and heavy Lake Michigan water in the air could never have achieved such sleepy lucidity without the actual six-stringed, sunburst manifestation before me.

Thus, to become a street musician. So simple, so obvious. Yet how does it happen? It's not exactly something you can study in night school, that destination I'm being urged toward by all sorts of random calling voices on the phone.

You Should Go To Night School.

Ok, hold on.

Is there an application to be filled out? Who should I list as references? In Chicago they say it's becoming some kind of union thing, complete with regulated hours and ID badges. Supposedly it's something I could just ask, but, you know – how to interrupt a song?

It hits me at once, her new strings shining seductive, soft in the wee hour, but really the seed was planted, the pipe dream of both a nothing and an everything idea, some years back. In New Orleans: Bloated, stuffed to the gourds on a roast beef po'boy and unnecessary beignets, with twilight growing purplish-orange over the Mississippi and the Natchez riverboat primed to sing her pipe song, strolling from Du Monde by myself, through the humidity, along the riverwalk, St. Louis Cathedral looming, casting her shadow across the square, café au lait in hand and a woozy feel to my stomach, a sluggish wobble in the knees. And before me, almost suddenly in the new quiet on the fringes of the Quarter, a man in a straw hat. Sideburns and goat, plaid shirt and cherry Martin-000. Strings uncut, billowing out the headstock like it needs a haircut. Sitting atop a milk crate of some sort. And slouching forward, with his right scraped boot keeping time, authoritatively under its own steam, seemingly.

"I've never been to heaven…" He was bellowing out, throaty, like the Wolf, his voice tumbling and barreling as if he took vocal lessons from the steel commuter train directly behind him as he faces the river. But really, facing only his guitar. More of a strummer than a picker, he still highlighted all the right blue notes, and it was a tasty 12-bars, with his right hand showing zero regard for the well-being of the strings, cuticles, or battered pick-guard.

…"But I've been to Oklahoma," his eyes closed in a grimace as he craned his neck toward the looming moon.

You're everything I want to be.

Sad, solo, unprofessional. Alone?

You have your guitar.

The true hurdle though, and there is always one, is the fact that few things in this world are more strangling, more pride-punching, more palm and pit greasifyin', blood-vessels-in-the-face-dilating, than picking in front of others. That slide, my move, really: third string second fret, up to the forth fret, hammer on the second string second fret, let the open e ring, double stop on the first and second strings, seventh and eighth fret, bend those fuckers, *beeeend* those fuckers. Thump the bass E. Simple. Slays me. Everytime, as soon as I pick up my baby. A perfect correlation to the very fiber of being. An entire temperament and worldview in a few notes and a couple of open strings in standard tuning. And in front of anyone that isn't one of my cats? Puny. Pathetic. Paltry. The sound surrenders all balls, all heart, all essence, all, fuck, all sound.

Something spiritual, ethereal, affirming is reduced to knobby, unknowing fingers on a cheapish Epiphone fretboard. This is all not to mention the plethora of flustered mistakes, that run out, my left hand fingers tripping over themselves like a drunk before a policeman, confounding matters with over-focus, while my right looks primed for a starring role in one of those failure to perform commercials.

Guess it took to about this point: my beard nearly fully half-filled in, zero callbacks, a spit-polished and re-polished resume holding every last morsel of self-worth in its carefully indented lines, my current pair of boxers down to the elasticity level of a burlap sack. Enough pride has been chiseled, enough red-faced shyness has been buried, overridden by pissed, echoing worthless uselessness. Enough with the perspective garnering, already.

The summer has started and by now, me and the Roommate have already played our end-of-start-of-summer game. The one where we cruise the old University grounds – the campus where we had met, split bags of pot, discussed books that weren't on syllabuses, made memories that we'd erase with booze later that same night, and forged a kind of bond, one with enough bank value to later tolerate paying rent to share a toilet seat and taco nights in these nascent years of not-quite adulthood.

We liked to pick a random Friday around 9, close to finals time, but after such student responsibilities, but also before mommies and daddies came with empty SUV's to pack Suzie and Aiden off back toward the suburbs and cushy internships and awkward hook ups with old high school flames in basements. And we'd find one of those end-of-year, end-of-the-world blowout keggers. Somewhere amongst our old stomping grounds: the crumbling clapboards that pass for not quite ghetto due to proximity to academic buildings, and the fact that pimply white kids with money, with their parents footing the rent bill via mail back in Des Moines, are only around for one year of boozing and condom-ed sex before the next, more adult place. So the slumlords can carry on, not make updates, and wait for the next batch of horny 20-year-olds who don't care about anything but a place to get loaded and occasional access to the library.

It used to surprise us how easy it was. To get in. To get a cup. To blend in a bit, but really it just being funny and us wanting it to be funny. To slouch in a shitty hallway and drink Busch and smoke cigarettes and let our ashes fall around the floor and think ourselves so superior before booking it back to the adult-ish part of town and bars where people sit down and drink decent, craft beer. But this year had been different. I had found myself separated from the Roommate, in an upstairs room, with a senior-to-be Journalism student with some acne but an endearing Hunter Thompson peyote-grip tattoo on his inner forearm - which had started up a conversation about writing, death, suicide, writing leading to death and suicide, etc. He had noted me grooving on the couch, maybe creeping, fawning over the fact that girls were actually dancing on the coffee table, something by Prince about fucking cranking quite loud while they gyrated. But this guy liked my bent, and I liked Hunter.

And suddenly there I was, with just a few brief answers about life, invited upstairs like a VIP. Like some old Will Burroughs type with an almost-beard and miles traveled and things seen - you could tell because I'd get that faraway look in my eye sometime.

"Wait, I read the paper, you're the guy that wrote that thinkpiece on that guy." Someone, in our pot-smoking party, name-dropping the weekly rag that almost passes for a capital-C 'career.' Aside from the money part.

"No. That was, uh… No. I don't write thinkpieces."

"But you're, like, published?" Someone else, a girl even, from the group that had gathered to take note of the great old man of letters who happened to be sitting in an attic bedroom, on the edge of a twin bed, surrounded by a cluster of early-20-somethings who looked skinny and sexy and had red streaks and expectant hunger in their eyes.

"I. Am. Published." Me, mustering gravity, nodding a bit humbly, thinking its been a while since I've turned in one of those 300-word opuses at 50 bucks a pop, affecting Pops-like cadence.

"Give us something, man, c'mon. Life guidance. Wisdom. Poetry!" Someone had passed me the bong, a footlong glass contraption with inlays and dank resin-y smell that can only come from college-y usage – so regular – and I was supposed to treat it like a microphone. Like a podium. Here was my commencement speech moment I always knew might come. And they were so full of rah-rah-ery. Disarming life boosterism. Positivity. Something creepy, sad about it all. Faraway from me. But I'd caught up a bit, at least tried, the blood coursing, the pot and beer chugging through the temples and warming the synapses, the about-to-speak loins. So it's all led up to now, I told myself. It's all led to now. They need you. Love you. Get 'em with the good stuff. The late night stuff of the road and the black and white pictures of you standing stoically full of philosophy and booze and smoking a cigarette with sad, straight face.

"Well, you see," me, pausing to clear my throat, for drama, and because dry mouth had begun her spit-sucking work... "All roads lead to nowhere. So choose one with heart."

"Huh."

Dead on arrival. Nothing. Polite nods and the blonde chick in the Stones T took the bong from my hand, needing something after my flop. Everyone suddenly avoiding eye contact, cackles subduing. So, I had searched, quick, not wanting to let it slip away:

"But really," here it comes, and they're back, "if you plan on fucking, don't drink whiskey. Because, you'll, like, get whiskey dick."

"Ahhh..."

With this I had them. A finer moment of collective group recognition I had not known. The honorary degree and robe seemed much deserved. The hats with the squares on top were suddenly ready to be tossed with enthusiastic malice toward the heavens. The lesson of a lifetime, delivered by the master, a guest of great, distinguished honor.

Later, me and the Thompson fellow had found ourselves outside, on his roof porch that was actually more like a fire escape. With Milwaukee's humble skyline blinking across campus, we smoked. I had won him, and he had won one of my Camels in return. He was even thinking about asking me to become a resume reference - he said nothing, but I could tell. And we were turning around life and I was thinking about venturing back down, to seek out the Roomate, to tell him of my speech-making powers, for us to sneak away and feel superior because we had almost more money and a bit more facial hair than these self-indulgent layabouts. But this fellow wouldn't stop with the questions.

"And you, like, know people, who have, like, actually died?" Him, so earnest, so green, much like someone I knew one time, from around these parts, maybe, though forever ago.

And me, with such mystical outline, shrouded in fog and smoke and grandpa-on-the-front-porch-ness. Taking a drag, exhaling, pondering, answering with tough repose: "Too many."

And now I think of him often, this fellow public performer with the Martin, and wonder if he's in the same spot, at this current moment, or back in the Quarter where I saw him, busking again, later that same night. Me with beer in hand now and a bit more gall, still not wanting to interrupt, or to be like all those tourist assholes with cargo shorts and directions to Bourbon Street. Pretending I got it, slouching back, getting it kind of, maybe. But certainly needing him to tell me, either way, just to be sure. Hoping maybe he would just stop, suddenly, mid-song, and see something kindred-like in my bloodshot eyes and low-pulled cap, spot it there before him. And then him, standing up off the milk crate, pointing at me, smiling that tobacco-stained smile, knowing my need, needing himself to take me under his wings and calloused, brown fingertips.

How do I do it?

You have your guitar.

But I don't know how.

You have your guitar, you have everything...

So I head for the top of the hill the morning after the sweaty Epiphone epiphany, before noon even. Blindly, quickly, without thinking too much, not even brushing my teeth, putting on my Aviators as to maybe detract the light of any kind of rational, clear-thinking. Assuring my ringing mom that I'm on the way to a job interview.

"What kind of company?"

"They travel around a bit."

"Like a sales position?"

"Like the circus."

"You're joining the circus?"

"Yeah – but not, more like a carnival."

"You're going to do something for a carnival."

"I'm hoping to be a ride-setter-upper."

And it is an interview, of sorts. So I drop the phone on my computer and close the apartment door on all things so technological, electrical. *And Ski, live and unplugged!* Down the street from my constant-shaded apartment. Near a bike path busy with joggers, some bikes. Atop a picnic bench. Not much traffic, but a bit more than my bedroom. Enough, at least, to warrant being there, amongst people, a silent corner performer, maybe there for himself (why the open case by his feet then?), maybe for some dough, for some supper. Whatever, amongst people, either way, acting as a member with contributions, offerings, even. Identity. Maybe. Humble as those bent notes and alternating bass lines may be. Flip-flops and rolled up jeans, lending a hint of Huck Finn insouciance, but the flatcap offering enough austerity, bluesman credibility, and a good shelter from human eyeballs.

And I play my 12-bars. *Back on the corner...* I hammer on, and pull off, my right hand slowly finding his behind-closed-doors cajones, my left hand clearing his head. *Singing the blues...* And me hammering on and pulling off, my voice rising, hitting the second string hard and the first ringing open, *I can see my reflection...* and the backbeat of my bass thumb thumping, a bit uneven, but solid enough... *in the shine of your shoes...* and I bend those treble strings, *beeeend*, and there's a melody in there somewhere, though it's simple, and I keep my head down and hammer on.

19

Sometimes, oftentimes, at least a couple of times a year, it is best, and downright necessary to take a good look at the pile of books, lists, corner dust bunnies, unchanged cat liter, sink of left-over pizza dishes, soiled stretched boxers on the floor next to the hamper, the whole general heap of your life stacked around you, and say, "Fuck it, I'm going to New Orleans." It could be one reason or the other: the sad dirty handkerchief nothingness of yet another cooling stained cup of coffee next to a blinking laptop screen. The unfruitfulness of an early morning schedule well maintained, yielding nothing but stifled yawns and another couple hours of sunshine hinting at itself, clearing it's throat, batting it's eyelashes – *ahem, see me? See my possibility?* – peering through the closed dusty blinds. It could be a roommate, stripping off shirt and tie in an exasperated huff before he's even through his bedroom door, then cracking a can of Schlitz and resigning to the couch's recesses with a hard-won and highly enviable *uhn't believedadayIhad* weariness, a TV baseball game and a deserved night of nothingness before him.

Or, in my case, it could be the notion - budding, taking root, reaching in the summer sun - that *I got this.*

Since the park that blinding day, and in the days and weeks thereafter – my fingers remembering their closed-door groove, my cheeks reducing their bloody self-consciousness bit by bit – a thumping resound has found its way back into my shoes. It might be the calves before me going by – always golden brown and tennis-court sculpted – sometimes acknowledging me in their Niked trot or walk, offering an oomph of validation, sometimes enough to allow a raised chin, up over the Epiphone, non-chalantly, non-commitally, but *there*, mutual acknowledgement. Then I'd lower it again in a casual nod of agreement, picking and thumping the whole time in my coolest sunglasses-on unaffectedness.

It might be the Rastafarian I saw at the start of week 2 of busker-dom, that first week of August, right after finding my usual wood-splintered spot on the picnic table top. Him with sunken cheeks, ratty dreads, stopping and stooping and pulling a register of Bugler, or something, from his satchel and sitting at my very table to roll his day's first smoke. Nodding my way, *and what was that? Was he actually grooving a little bit there?* A slight hike in the general shoulder region, a drop, his chin jutting forward methodically, then retracting. The excitement is enough that I have to look down, again, quick. Losing time, finding it with a self-deprecating smirk toying across my cheeks. Thinking less, bending more... *Is he dancing?* I can't look, can't ponder, or else, shit, yep, there goes time again. Tap your foot now and keep tapping. It might be that somewhere along the timeline of me like this, head craned in creative consternation, lost in a flow, minutes out of days becoming worldly events in and of themselves, I stumble suddenly back to the realm of drop-D tuning. There it is, *there...* just a three-quarters tune of the low E knob, and *bbbrrrrr*. Echoing, like the voice of my worst hangover, emanating from the back of a too-many-cigarettes throat. But with something to say, not back to sleep on a Sunday morning, but with places to go, an insistence, no time to lose.

And that must be it. The reverberation carries me away from that picnic table back to the woodshed of my apartment. And then back again. And then again, the next day. This time with no hat on and no restraint in the bellow of my voice. Even recalling some Dave Van Ronk. Something is gleefully obscene about the whole thing, the remembrance of classics trumping reenlistment back toward the human race. No matter either way. Not when that slide is executed so well, when I can glance to the heaven's like I was Lightnin', in pained bluesman exasperation. The alternating D bass line by now underlining what feels like a new breath, a new pulse, the sound of me walking in slow motion through a Wes Anderson flick. Steel resonating against fretted rosewood, pulsing and rattling suddenly-insomniac cells. It carries over to the keyboard too, where job sites are minimized, forgotten and sentences suddenly begin to snake, flow. The glow of the screen is warm again, friendly. An old pal: *Hey, 'member when...* Me, sitting there at night, with five calloused left fingers and one sore right thumb and pointer, the whiteness beginning to fill itself up. No more resume adjectives, though. Only pure, serious magic. Even punctuation and the desire for coffee digress back toward afterthought.

By week three I'm feeling like an outrider on day two, enough removed from tough hesitations and long goodbyes, with anxiety and fatigue mixing into a dreamy swell of possibility. Teeming, careful apathy has become my new, consuming ambition.

Inertia has been achieved, gained, increased exponentially just since last Tuesday. When not on my tabletop, there I am, in the green chair. Door shut on the Pabst-swilling Roommate, leaving him in the dark as to the whole, natural, necessary new course of things. How could I explain? But to tell him how little I'm now stopping to use the handy wooden back-scratcher and stare blankly at the dead-spider-blotched walls. Maybe he could tell, if the job-holding indifference would let him. Maybe, if he listened, it'd be obvious by the reduction in *slurrrp*, and the increase in *tink-tink-tink* audibly filling the ether around me. *Tink-tink-tink.*

I'll give em something to read, those pricks!

No way of telling who I mean by *pricks*, but they're out there, around that corner, sipping at the next table, at the other end of my emails, laughing longshoremen back in mean Frisco bars demeaning my carefully-chosen plaid. They are all over the endless vestiges of the callous, vacuous world know as the Internet. Thus windows are closed, ignored, narrative is laid out, metaphored, twisted – just get it down, anything but a description of the sky.

So, the calamity has been bridged, ridden over and rendered stale in its annoying longevity. At a certain point, if he's no casualty, a victim of tragedy becomes a survivor. Once, I took a spill down some stairs: a hazy fall night in Kansas City, a long day's drive and too many Fat Tire's, a friend's brother's unfamiliar house, an unfortunately situated cat. A welt, a hematoma, a baseball-sized lump of some or another name formed on my left shin, substituting for what should have been a cracked skull and a trip in a hearse. As an unhealed week turned into a year, self-consciousness became regret. As a year turned into 3 and this lump, this thing, this mass of blood and muscle on the wrong side of my calf, became a part of me, lament turned into a sort of nostalgia. Like that: unsightly nuisance, worn with a badge of pride. Unemployment and the world's heaping indifference has become my battle scar.

Along with Unemployment checks.

In your face, Severance!

But, remember, you were so excited?

Not anymore – 2 year limit on this shit!Haaha!

But I never asked anything, not even a filing...

Yeah, that was good.

Not even an application.

Yeah... Nice...

And that day, you didn't know if you could afford a pizza, and then, there I was at midnight, no trip to the bank. Because I knew you were ever so hungry.

Yeah, well, we did have some crazy times...

I flash on the office, the clamor thick and yawns pervasive, someone else's ass grazing, farting in the crevices of my old trusty chair. Or maybe my chair is now in storage, collecting dust, rust, forgetting my manly essence of cheesesteak toots like I was never even there. And here, suddenly, assuredly, I'm readying my shoulder, flexing, prepping a resting spot for the rucksack. Rolling up my jeans with pride, *hallelujah I'm a bum again*. And I'm back to the cabinet for a reload of beans. Fattening myself in every way now. I feel like picking a direction, away from all such wasted professionalism, way away. Obviously, maybe only to me, maybe because one of the compass points has been covered and there's only three left and one of those is boring, but obviously - South.

The words and the bench and the calves going by and all those words can wait. Rest here, marinate, settle, mature in that oily, succulent stew I've crafted. For a moment of clarity deserves recognition, and something is yet to be sought elsewhere. Mistakes and waste notwithstanding, a corner has been turned, breached, and now there is only a muck of further research before me. More forward movement, into the *muck*.

With everyone I know still urging me toward earlier bedtimes, I can already feel the future melancholy for my current days. When the endless cups of office coffee and computer screens and desperate smoke breaks and numbing invoices and niceties and pleasantries and endless strings of Monday mornings will override me and my handkerchief. All those inevitable things await. And my eyes will sweat for the now gone possibility of a train on the west coast, a Tuesday night bender, a long, lazy trip down south. Everyone yearning for me to find a way to fill my days, and every fiber is screeching for more night.

There is never enough night, but, in New Orleans, at least there is more. And as an abstract concept to me now, from my green chair, as I'm prepping Orbitz to act as benefactor yet again, giddy rationalization comes easy and natural. The heap of guitars and sentences and life messiness around me warrants both escape and reward. Two things at once. *At once!* And she's down there: my two things, both a lush-voiced lover and a filthy-mouthed, scab-ridden whore. Soon, there will even be double fisting, on the streets, me with tears of gladness and grins twisted with gloom. That French-Carribbean-Black American smorgasboard of laxidasical craziness. Nahlins, naawlins, norleans, New Orleans, mon amour, the only city I'd speak French for, so many things, the only city whose mere utterance and notion makes the hair on the back of my neck stand up and water start at the corner of my eye.

20

Recognition can be a funny thing. Like, there you are, in Uptown New Orleans with a conglomerate roast beef, cheese, tomato, mayo, hot-sauce-drowning French bread monstrosity literally fucking your face, deep-sixing the very integrity of your throat, with greasy lettuce wisps leaving a snail's trail of juice across your lips, fingers, and the butcher paper so helpless, weak, strained and stained on the formica table below. With the entire essence of being alive at the moment contained within your mouth's loving reaction to that which it is being penetrated by, so mercilessly, so blatantly sloppy. With nothing to think of, nothing blinking in your head, save, *easy, don't choke* and *dear God, don't let that meat fall out the back!* Afraid to set it down, your quivering elbows out at weird angles, fingers clawed for dear life, but still, somehow, delicately loving, so great is the anxiety over structural disassembly. And the combo of this here joint's friendly, divey laxness and a newly discovered indifference toward personal hygiene or appearance combine in a sated portrait of contented, insouciant gluttony. *Do whachya wanna* echoes in my head when I come to recognize myself in all this outside-of-body, second person narrative bliss, when the everythingness of the world is simple and impossibly complex, both, and there it is, resting right behind the front teeth. With my stomach pining, reaching up in a sort of gastrointestinal act of sexual arousal. And everything gone through today, from the 6am alarm to a life-pondering trip to the airport. To the God-fearing Chicago cab ride, 90 down I-94 and no blind spot checks, whatsoever, to the Big Bad O'Hare, to the inevitable sweaty pits and 600 miles-an-hour, to the bus all the way down Magazine. (And why is it that buses in other cities are so frighteningly foreign to me? Like it's a big deal.

As if their different from my daily home mode of transportation, as if I'll get on and legitimately not be able to figure out where to put the money. All the passengers laughing aloud in their collective localness). And a little belch escapes and I'm only pleased by the additional spatial allowance, surprised, like finding a parking spot on a congested Friday night downtown, ready for more, even a tad hungered by the noxious taste of the gas as it leaves the mouth.

Yes, there he is. I know *this* guy. With the mayo coating the chin whiskers and Delta sweat on the brow. Loving the meat-and-bread threesome like he's never loved a woman, never even thought about a woman outside of that confusing pubescent dreamscape that caused the out-the-window throwing of a perfectly good pair of checkered boxers in that strange middle school state. Alone and blissful in an Uptown sandwich shop. Surrounded with neighborhood workers and a hairy-armed UPS driver talking loudly to the proprietor about the mayor, peppering sentences with 'yeah you rights,' all taking breaks to satiate, render sustenance for additional energy to shuffle more papers, offer more formalities, answer more phones, pass more days and pay more bills, get back behind the mule in whatever manner. And then there's this guy, plaid shirt newly spotted with Louisiana hot sauce, a crumpled Word document on the table next to his Abita, furtively eyeball-consuming his surroundings, sweating, with his consciousness leaning forward toward the next bite. Finding an *end*. Between all those warm-blanket layers of warm beef. The safe cave yearned for in childhood. A position in and of itself. A fatty, dirty, dimly-lit place.

The road careening toward the colon.

Face already aglow with post-sex glisten, I'm swiping the corners of my mouth with the back of my hand, trying to clear any interferences for the precious, inevitable last few noshes, when I recognize another guy. *That* guy is Ivan Neville.

"Hey... man." Me, back to being cool and my first utterance

since 'roast beef, dressed.'

"Yeah you right." Ivan, sauntering through the door and toward the counter with the familiarity of a man who knows his way around a po' boy shop. Who knows his way around a po' boy.

Trying to remember, this is Art's son, no, it's Aaron's son, no... suddenly he's sitting by me, and we're talking meats like fat kids at the loser table in lunch. The author of so many nights of my own brain cell genocide, of 5am bouts of soul-tiring, head-nodding, white-boy, dusty-floored and tin-ceilinged honky-tonk grooving, of being up till not when the sun is coming up, but when the sun is so fully realized as to punch you in the head as soon as you hit the door, and make you instantly wonder why in fuck's sake no one has ever introduced New Orleans to 'bar time.' Like that, we are comparing notes. Him in his Sopranos t-shirt and baseball cap pulled low, meaty forearms the same color as my sandwich's dripping gravy debris.

"You're from here, right?"

"Sure."

Me, now pretending as if I was not looking for a pen to jot down notes on meat approaches: note the napkin technique. Him, literally saving face with a simple scrunched-in-the-palm grip of paper. Steadying the big ship toward, and then away, from his lips with one assured, veiny hand. I'm wondering if he'll wash them tonight before taking a seat behind the organ. Wondering if it'd be weird to ask.

All of this could have been Parasol's, it could have been Guy's, it could have been a number of others, so fully realized each is as to be of a lot, and so completely different from one another and from anything in all the Seattles and Chicagos and bullshit desperate, pesky cities of progression and striving and achieving. And just like that I've up and saddled that indefinability that is this place. It's the strange, surprising otherness of a glimpse behind the curtains. A look of the innermost gears interlocking, by some impossibly engineered Swiss design, running on it's own sense of self, or something. Smiling to myself a smile that mocked all that is right, straight. Back home seems suddenly decades away. It only took a trip to lunch. He hasn't mentioned his gig tonight, and neither have I. Watching the gravy pool with the red Louisiana on the paper before me, shaping into faceless Midwestern states, I wonder what to do with the rest of my day.

What I'm looking for, and also, not looking for – other than any traces of Kurtz, down the river – is twofold, and sketchy even to myself. On one hand is the fella with the Martin, obviously, with the hat and that gig bag full of secrets, waiting, for me, by the Mississippi or on the streets. I'll turn off Toulouse and he'll be there, facing upriver by St. Peter, his back to me, but now suddenly rising off the crate. Mid-song, not stopping, just slowing the beat, lifting the guitar, turning slowly and looking at me over the shoulder with a devilish and knowing smirk... *I just wanna see his face.* If I listen close enough, the thump of his low E will carry, call me home, escorted by the humidity, that dense slowing thing, the same heaviness that schooled Louis. Showing me the this, and the that, too.

So, I trail him, all over that city. From Carrolton to Frenchmen and back again, stopping to lean, somewhat French-like and somewhat pimp-like, against lightposts to adjust my aviators, and wipe the sweat from my now-pimply forehead. And to absorb. Mostly, to absorb. The fluidity of to-go cups carrying me down late-night streets, and through the pressing-down wetness. Wondering why I don't live here, wondering what it would take not to feel this. Conjecturing that a castrated man of severe blindness and a touch of the flu could easily, with no extemporaneous effort, still get it – would still want to root for the Saints.

And I trail her, too. Not wanting to remind myself, not wanting to think of Kurtz's drawings, but doing it anyway. The idea being that the words marinating and stewing back home need more direction, more heart, more oomph. *Research that shit, Ski, Research.* This was, after all, a business trip. A business *venture*. And a story of high-minded seriousness and poetry, of a man searching for the last woman his dead friend ever slept with: an Ebony seductress of voodoo great and unknown, a high priestess of 'nawlins gris gris, holding at once the sultry, veiled secrets about the last days and the current incarnation of the departed. Something like that needs a touch of verisimilitude. Freshness. Something. At least a side of properly spiced red beans.

Thing is, when somebody leaves, when it's the day after Christmas, and you sit on the driver side and watch your brother pull his ass off the passenger seat in the rushed melee of the O'Hare Departures lane, you wonder why X-mas eves and their never-ending glut of Goose Island and whiskey and pot and chesty laughs under the sparkling lights come so infrequently. And you want to go back there – just a few hours ago it was! - and not to the normalcy and the routine. The numbness and yawns and the *how was your holiday?*'s At this point there is, in certain men, the need for a good goodbye, for a period on the brilliant, dying sentence. When you're not going to see somebody for an indefinite period of time. Well then, what about when it's an all too definite period of time? When the last image is but a mental one, and it's your friend's feet hovering, toes pointing and yearning for the dirt, for the wood on a back deck on a crisp, foggy California morning. For anything other than the miserable, warbly nothingness of the fragile wind? Then, the myth of The Big Send Off gets an upgrade, from wistful, shoulder-shrugging begrudging acceptance, to downright, fist-clenched imperativeness. *This is what happened.*

And so like I figure business trips probably go, I find myself sulking over a glass of Dewars, the ice clinking, in a sweaty, dark, vine-walled bar courtyard off of Decatur Street. In the dingy outside bathroom is currently resting a dead cockroach, and as the bladder has filled, I've been in to see him. Peter-in-hand, letting the alcohol flow from whence it came, the Gulf I suppose, but getting the toilet seat too, I cock my head and keep one eye on the bastard both to make sure he doesn't spring forth and come at me, and to listen to what he might have say.

*So, my buddy had a lady down here, I'mma...*Me, never knowing how to start these kinds of conversations.

You're looking for her? Roach, still on back, legs still in air, still not moving.

Shit, I thought you were dead.

She's the one that's dead.

No. You're confused.

Am I?

Hours later, some bars are shuttering and some are just coming to life, a fresh round of hungry livers released from uniformed entrapment at the casinos, four-star hotels, and, yes, other bars. And I'm on Chartres and lousy with drink and a shrimp po'boy, with cheese, is dangling in plastic by my side, and a tall can of sweating Bud is in the other, and I'm making-out, hard, with a never-ending Camel, and a sweat stain along my spine, underarms, and pretty much everywhere that isn't my teeth grows like an oil slick under and up through my gray t-shirt. And the distant room, crisp with bright cable TV and AC, at once feels so rewarding, and too far away from the right now. From the standing under this rickety balcony as a soft rain starts and finishes before my eyes. At home I rarely see a reason pressing enough to want to get out of bed. And here, I can't see one sufficient to go toward it.

But the day, that dirty leper, is creeping in, intruding, pushing me toward the sheets and pillow with a callous, heavy hand. Someone should have locked her out, but all are welcome here someone seems to say. I consider another bar, a corner number on Royal where the action is centered around a short row of video poker games and one of Ivan's relatives of some sort is belting about the moon - singular and distinctive to these parts – through the jukebox. The ubiquitous fizz of bottles of Abita opening in chorus behind him. By this point though, there is no stopping that whore of sunrise. I cross the street, but she beats me to the other side, gaveling forward with hand out, asking something, taking the deliciousness right out of the Budweiser and replacing it with a tugging regret, rationality. Also a realization, and the dreadful before-bed, drinking-headache. Clinging yet to the dying night, I'm still looking, but knowing - She was never really there. God jokes with his best ones.

Long and short of it: The magic of our last night, it really ended just like this one here – save for a different all-night po' boy shop and then a drunken faceplant on a dirty shag carpet in a rented slave's quarters Uptown. Me, I made the couch at least, in my grinning stupor. And the two of us, that late spring night, our hours spent bouncing on rickety barroom floors and smiling rounds bought for one another, they were good. But not sufficient to my story. To the climax. To what the tale needed and what was told to myself before this day began asserting her bitchy self. The Big Send Off was in truth, as flaky as last week's French bread, deserving of the trash at least, but merely sitting discarded, on the ground, soaking in so much Bourbon Street hurl. It's unbelievable what you can see through such haziness, through the growing humidity and mean-spirited light, but I recognize, painfully, now. Like a city bursting to view through the sudden last cloud layer on a plane's descent, I see. Emptiness below. The only city is an empty, waiting bed. Followed by hangover reality. That ebony goddess of New Orleans, they chatted. A drink was bought, drank, a handshake and that was it. But the guardian of the flame for my friend's way-gone soul, she never existed. And so I'm pushed toward bed.

Part 3

21

Freedom, when packaged in the form of a fall, when served unsuspectingly straight no chaser, direct to the gut, when offered void of strings or nets, the way it should only hang in a poem, maybe, or possibly the Pledge of Allegiance, is not always a good thing. Quite the opposite, in personal takes, though maybe I've just been burnt through experience. There was, of course, the aforementioned down-the-stairs tumble. In Kansas City, that silliest of all cities. Where a most-of-the-day drive in a rented SUV, alongside a less-than best-friend, with all efforts to impress a girl of calves so sumptuous they might as well been have been dipped in honey, had been met with joyous beers, a tour of downtown, the finest in dank Midwestern pot, and then me, just barely after midnight, flailing at the top of a darkened set of basement stairs like a confused Special Olympics swimming entrant. As if I had just been met by Norman Bates' mother, surprised, stabbed, arms suddenly sent in a desperate back pedal through the air, feet a-stagger and gasping for a hold, stomach (full of barbecue, because what is else is there *really* to do in Kansas City?) barreling toward the throat and mouth in some kind of anti-gravity neutralizing response, head, with entirely too much time to contemplate how it all might end. But far worse than bodily damage: a vague feeling, as I plummeted helplessly, arms behind me in futile protest, Oh-face across the lips, of looking entirely uncool, untogether, and *un* just about everything I'd driven 8-plus hours to achieve.

I had always been averse to such experience, even more so than most, I suppose, since a well-meaning second grade teacher – one whom waddled, believably, maybe just in a career-long attempt to sell this story, maybe just because of a borderline grotesque extra girth she carried below the torso – had related her grisly tale of a broken tailbone. It was the result of some nefarious miscreant, probably in an outlandish attempt at flirting or maybe rape, pulling the chair out from under her about-to-sit ass. Despite her admonishments and continuous hobbled patrols around the classroom, for much of those days the *ohshitwheresmyseat* game was still a rage, and always an act of heralded cleverness. We'd all bust up and the target's face would turn crimson, and palms would get instantly sore and red and need to be clapped and dusted against one another to remove that ubiquitous elementary-school floor grime, and heads would turn toward the point of commotion. The relative ripple effect waning as it spread out toward the more distant views and cheaper seats. Everyone wanting to be a part, in on it; aside from the floored sap, whom now, as if it wasn't bad enough, had to stand upright, emerge from the forest-like cover of rows of desks, had to, and make his disheveled body erect, announcing to the audience with ruby cheeks and sheepish aw shucks grin, that, *yes, indeed, I am the schmuck here.*

Like rednecks in a barroom brawl, bloodily and violently flailing at their own misinterpreted limitations, reaching for something, what childhood tomfoolery, when shaken and contained in the carbonation of schoolroom confinement, can espouse.

Only one time though, in the brief, unremarkable realm that I would consider my adult life, had I had the chair so irrevocably, so terminally, so all-at-once yanked from under an expectant ass. It was rather a comfy chair at that, and, albeit removed from Mrs. Greene's oafish attempts to curb such shenanigans, it was positioned at a distance I had long deemed safe enough from the hooligans, uncertainty, and crippling embarrassments of youth. Especially when you consider that said chair had wheels, some kind or another of imitation leather, and not one but two of its very own lumbar support levers. I mean, at this advanced level of status-gained, comfort-earned and butt-cushioned importance, should one still be looking over his shoulder?

Well, not everytime you sit down, *but…*

And then you're red-faced and dusty-palmed and hopeful your tailbone pain isn't the season-ending variety, and with any luck you weren't just on the way back from the break room because then there's probably fresh, black office coffee spewed in about one thousand directions, not enough of them away from your face. When all you wanted was to sit down, punch up some more random, insipid dot com's, dial in some tuneage on the headphones, look busy and mildly annoyed like any self-respecting office professional, and quietly, defiantly push your actual responsibilities back a bit more, while you still know, yes, they are there, dreadful but protecting like some kind of bug spray kept under the kitchen sink.

But to anyone that's ever had the seat pulled out from under them, well, even those who haven't, and even when the seat-pulling fails to result in a shattered coccyx or coffee scalds, it's quite obvious that there's no good way to stick the said chair back in. Only time can repair: the toppled or skewed sitting apparatus is realigned, a sore fanny is rendered sheepishly back in place, face capillaries return to their normal size, laughs recede back into classroom stoicism. We all become friends again. Even the unfurled spirit and that evil, cunning, chair-pulling hand. Such is the normal, natural unsaid progression of things. Operating like my cats lick themselves, unthinking, knowing. In the right direction for the right purposes. But do those instincts stay with us, all the long trek into adulthood? I mean, it's been awhile since participating in this game. Do they go too into the tangling, unseemly messiness of unemployment?

By the time the call comes, summer's light and any passion for it have begun to decline and wilt like a whore with too much experience. This is great and all, but, *enough*. Enthusiasm fades, time passes. Of course not fast enough for the words to begin putting themselves down, like I had hoped, like I had envisioned transpiring in a rousing cinematic montage, flourishing, basking, curlycueing in their own poetic meter. Not quite quick enough for the calloused fingertips to begin leading themselves, effortlessly, fluidly up and down the fret board like they were dancing around notes that already existed. Uncontrollably though, summer is dying. And the phone is ringing. Waking me from the deep, pleasantly-damned sleep of the jobless. Another in a long string of collective Sunday mornings.

"Hello." Me, intonation implying statement, one far from a question. It's a bit after 11am, the sun, rather annoyingly, is shining, and I start in after a trapezoidal eye crust from my left socket corner.

"Ski!" The caller ID might as well have registered 'Reality', but had it and there would be no way I'd have answered, no way I'd find myself like this, cradling the Motorola in one hand, propped up on an elbow.

"How can I direct your call." No question mark, or so I imagine. A slight smile forming though, unconsciously, but the booger, shocking in its perfect manifestation of the color 'sepia,' maintains most of my groggy focus.

"What have you been up to?" The voice, associated with a face I'd like to say, maybe even believe, that I haven't thought of in some seven months. Not since I pummeled it, endlessly, mercilessly, like Tyson, in a barrage of under-breath four letter words. Cursed it with a vagabond's forlorn misery – hateful of the insider's ugliness, but spiteful at the condemnations toward an outsider.

"Sleeping." Me, a yawn escaping, unsuppressed. My hand wandering below the blanket and below the border, satiating, unabashedly, the morning's ostentatious itch.

"You been working?"

"You didn't hear? I lost my job."

Har-har. But there's a tentativeness to the laugh that almost disarms me, so far removed is it from our usual Monday-over-coffee ribbings of each other's respective football teams. Where I would set my mug down next to the shipping computer as soon as he first emerged from the back office, and I'd whirl past him in a Barry Sanders-patented spin move, break through the imaginary linebackers, and then turn to come back at him (the warehouse area not being wide enough for full field re-creation), hand extended in full, intimidating stiff-arm pose, all while play-by-playing breathlessly in my best Marv Albert... Where we would begin with chesty shit-talkings, me panting in work boots and flannel after my histrionics, hand on forehead, incredulous about one thing or another from the previous day's NFL proceedings, before catching my breathe, and – if he happened in a jocular-enough mood – fake-juking and tearing off down the sidelines, miming an over the shoulder catch and bursting with effusive F-bomb jubilations now in the vain of the color commentator. Mr. Boss Man, grinning and shaking his head. Where I would picture him, endearingly, in pj's, on the couch, all the day before, planning his little nuanced observations of the 3-4 put-downs of my squad. Laughing that knowing boss laugh, of comfortable but friendly aloofness. Me, not brown-nosing but still scoring points, crossing goal lines.

The call, I can tell, he carefully choreographed. Since 8 this morning, perhaps. A part of me cries out to change the rhythm, cut-in, double-time the song. Blitz.

"Seriously, Ski, what are you up to?"

"Oh ya know, no chair, been doing lots of squatting..."

Surprise, yes. But a part of me has been waiting. And I can feel something else: Bridges long-crossed, some of them burned, crumbled, or downright forgotten, each getting a good once over from a third party, some earnest, fresh-outta-college crew cut engineer.

He's probably taking the case pro bono, just to salt the wounds.

Ahh, nothing here we can't fix. The engineer, fixing his glasses.

Really, you can tell that? Me, with bed-head, in disbelief.

I have my degree.

I have my degree, and I don't know dick.

"You want to come to work on Monday?

Just like that. Before I can even think to think 'here it comes.' I feel power slipping from my tires, the back end coming out, like when you know you shouldn't hit the brakes in snow, but you do. Control replaced by some kind of unsubstantiated wave of release, of nerve-end tingling. Of it's *outtamyhands*. And it doesn't seem quite real. Like the long-prepared for moment of asking her out, finally, of knowing you are doing it and are right there in the middle, yearning for a distance when you can look back at the unanimous peaked hugeness of this moment, when it will become a memory. A hurdle, crossed successfully or not, either way though, one to be looked at with a deep exhale, a perceptive smirk and the assuredness of wisdom-gained. But I'm not really sure what is to be decided, what to be done.

I do know it's as if my perceptions are the only reality, and the swirl of society, etc. is but a cool creek's stream, one with which I can easily pull both dangling feet from. Maybe still a bit cold upon retraction, but they'll dry, they'll dry. I note the eye booger, now dropped on the bed sheets, glinting in a ray of sun sneaking through the shut blinds, and I middlefinger-flick the fucker as hard as possible – even winding-up the fist a bit – toward the crevice between bed and wall.

"Well, I'll have to check my dayplanner."

"-."

"But I know there's one more thing I have to do."

" - "

"I have to take one more trip."

"..."

"My grandmother's dying."

"Oh, jeez, I didn't..."

"And I have to go to New York."

Silence. Carrying, speckled silence. The sound of a man undone mid-stride. Tripped by an unexpected uneveneess in the sidewalk. It feels neither good nor bad, simply like I caused it.

Like a lost friend, here comes momentum again, sweeping me as it did in those pre-summer days of hopeful, aimless Faulkner-reading, like that old heroic 'lazy man', lifting me out of the sheets and my contented through-the-boxers ball-scratching and toward the ever-increasing ass-grooves of my green chair. As soon as I say it – and isn't that the way it has to go? – I know it, feel it, there in the itchy ripples of my loins to be true.

I leave him with a vague notion of a call back, he leaves me with a semi-pressing sense of being needed. But the leaving trunk has already been effortlessly unruffled, garnered again from the closet annals. *Just don't take me to Kansas City*, the ol' pal seems to be saying. *'Cuz this might be it...* With this we're both silent. Even the cats, waged in some kind of one-on-one genocide in the next room, seem to suddenly simmer. A hush of reckoning settles over the whole dusty dark apartment. And I wonder what day it is and how I can continue to receive unemployment checks if back amongst the working, contributing, lunatic masses. A plane reverberates some-where overhead, going, someplace else. Feeling less titillating than before, the sound is more like the foreboding of what I imagine to be my future background noise. Of the rustle overhead of other people taking-off and leaving, bound for Paris, bound for... and me in my clean shirt, showered and deodorized, headphones on, looking for escape only in the wires leading from the work desktop to each ear.

No, old friend. Me, almost actually talking aloud to the worn gray rucksack, it's stitching frayed in parts, no-name brand spelled in white letters now sullied by airplane bowel stains and skidmarks, random city maps crinkled and hastily-folded in her side compartments, tattered airline tags still adorning the tough handle.

This we do up right. This one we make count.

22

She would be a long, dusty, grueling trip – the way I wanted. Beans would be rationed. Shirts would be sullied. Road-stubble sprouted and worn like a badge. Meandering down through big-dicked Chicago, I'm changing buses amidst the over-compensating skyscrapers in the bustling, autumn-coming blowing of the Loop. Bounding off of one 94 East-barreling Greyhound for another in front of Union Station – austere, foreboding, mysterious and beautiful in his inner-potentiality for spewing a willing traveler in any of countless directions out, over the heartland. California Zephyr? Empire Builder? *City of New Orleans, all aboooard...* But no time for that now, for gazing at the glowing digitized 'Departures' screen, all fantasizing and soul-leaning. For I'm out on Canal Street, ignoring and moving past the new driver who's shepherding his flock of wheeled suitcases and baby strollers, gentlemanly assisting with the pushing-in of retractable plastic handles, making sure a barely-vertical octogenarian couple doesn't topple and faceplant off the tall city curb while waiting to board. Noting my rucksack he head-motions in the direction of the under-bus storage, the unknowable bowels. Rendering my printed ticket at arm's length, eye-contacting and nodding assuredly, I flip the big bag over a beefy shoulder, and wordlessly mount the stairs in an inarguable, rugged act of purpose and direction.

Finding the spot nearest the bathroom, I plop in the aisle seat, fold hands peacefully across my little beer-bulge, pull flat cap low over the eyebrows, open mouth in a scowling almost-snore pose, and immediately feign a deep sleep. If the bus fills up, or half fills up, strangers coupled with strangers in those insufferable arm-rest unions which by hour two inevitably turn acrimonious, well then,

I'm in the best spot to remain solo. Most, surprisingly, are unwilling to wake a sleeping bus-er, and with the seat's leaving so little leg room, there is no way to scooch past without a blatant disruption. There *is* still some decency in the world. And so, we'll be halfway to Gary before I open my eyes, yawn, and stretch my arms in an exaggerated motion out to the heavens and then the sides. Room to breathe as I take it in: Chicago's southside street names turning into numbers, then turning into numbers reaching very high, into the 100's, before melding into a bridged wasteland of hulking, hard-looking steel, all of it moving backward through my unimpeded window view.

Bus. Why a bus? Why a bus, indeed, anyone with the misfortune to book one of the long-distance variety out of Chicago, and sit rigid, knees to chin, practically offering oneself a hummer, has certainly come to ask by the time Indiana rolls around. But here it is direct and purposeful, and time, of the essence. Namely the defiant wasting and play-doh-like stretching of time: The final existing amidst time outside of time, the dayplanner intentionally avoided, the itinerary bullet-pointed on a Word document simply with day #'s and not with names. No 'Monday,' 'Wednesday' for this go-round. But the schedule is also hardly more than a skeleton, more than an arrow pointing down the road – everything after the words 'Milwaukee to Chicago 7:15am' and 'Chicago to Buffalo 9:15am' seeming to pale in importance. The miles becoming the desired effect in themselves. That bottled up feeling of a bus seat like my own version of a monk's abstinence. Chastity. Asceticism. Working toward enlightenment, earning it, trying, maybe.

Of course all of this is hindsight, blinded sopping romantic bullshit and even Kerouac must have seen that, at some point, eventually. Here, from the keyboard where a fresh cup of coffee is only the next-room away, and next to that is the beatific respite for my oft-beleaguered colon, with the loud vent and louder faucet and the books creating sanctuary. And the bed is just over yonder, almost within arm's length, and I can really call a halt to this day, this movement, whenever I wish. From this distance though, all that road dust and lean days of cramped-leg strife seem to hold something, something eternal, holy. But when that too-long-sitting feel creeps into each central-cheek butt muscle, and you idle alongside the diesel-smelling beast on desperate smoke breaks in Buttfuck, Ohio, gazing at vacant fields and gas price signs, and you think, then know, that, yes, you can absolutely smell that lady across the aisle's moist flatulence, bus travel is haggard and awful in the worst way. So, what: all for the feel of sitting back, letting someone else steer, make my decisions for me, *please*, plodding along in my boxers while the striving creased pants of the world keep a foot pressed to their respective gas pedals, allowing for the river to do it's downstream flowing, unimpeded. For who am I to impede? One last time, these last few hours, this last carefree itinerary, maybe, I won't.

The course is set, and along the way there is an Amish family - no, not 'till the distant Deliverance-hills of ol' gray Pennsylvania – but there they are, waiting, their stinky homemade pilgrims outfits violently arguing with me in my head. *Yo ZZ, y'alls ever heard of Old Navy?* There is the crucial iPod playlist of bus songs, *Hey bus driver, keep the change,* and the budding, ebullient bounce of Bruce, nascent and earnest in his first effort, is deliriously infectious, inspiring, then, briefly, crippling as I suddenly reflect on his dreaded nickname. A remembered, feared notion. An old and hoary one I had been comfortably on vacation from. Universally and daily accepted, but my existence a permanent state of those magic old Friday states when the 'boss is outta town,' and collars can be loosened thusly. There is the pertinent – maybe too-obvious? – cracked-spine Kerouac, laid out on my sleepy lap. And there is time: to gaze, to grow a voracious in-the-pits hunger, to contemplate what I will do to a set of tacos upon arrival in my hometown, and to contemplate that old place itself. Whirring and whooshing through the rain toward Cleveland, enjoying the evident long sadness and sad longness of the Midwest, a region defeated, somehow. A land of roadside cows and Detroits. Flatness and corn. Akron's, Erie's, and non-descript Indianapolis'. A homogeneous section I'm growing more a part of everyday, I think. On toward Buffalo in the growing darkness, and the land itself seeming to take note. To rise and come interesting, somewhat, with hints of altitudes and terrain, as a State of relevance, of things happening, of fashion and a big city, *the* big city, inches closer. Or so New York seemed to me, when first Midwest-relocated, and in my early gasps of telling people where I was from that glint that would come into their eye, that 'here is a man of importance' ray in the broadening of the sockets. And you'd like to keep it going, but there is no choice but to stop it: No, no, nowhere near the City, no, no, I know I don't have an accent, no, no it's way in *Western* New York, no, no, almost apologetically, I'm from Buffalo.

Buffalo: Detroit without the glamour, roughhewn, scabrous, taking on a quality of gray in every facet of life that might appear most effective in a post-apocalyptic flick set in the hills of the Ukraine. Actually existing in a perfect microcosm of itself within the tired walls of the downtown bus station. With winners nowhere really to be seen, lots of homely resignation, Bills logos sported in unfashionable ways, with something more like irony than pride. Teeth yellowed with Marlboros and guts fattened by Canadian brews and lovingly fried chicken wings. No business suits, anywhere – even less than at the Cleveland station. An obscene amount of hawks waiting to offer me a ride, or what probably seems an obscene amount because there are any. For whoever is rolling into Buffalo on a bus can only be returning home, and thus, have a car, or ride. And the suitcase skids all over the cheap looking floors, seeming to indicate a hastily beaten path out of town. Pointing the way, really. And me, paddling back upriver now, sensing Kurtz or something like him. Getting back to the core. Through the bus terminal purgatory, and back outside, the air has assumed a distinctly between-seasons flavor, the growing chill on the wind mingles with a lingering humidity. Neither here nor there. I hail a taxi. Or rather, I enter the first of three that immediately angle toward my person as soon as I'm through the sliding doors.

"Mighty Taco, please." Me, with the words I've waited all day, all year in fact – since my last time here – to say.

"Which location, there's like 12 now." Him, the 'now' indicating his immediate recognition of a local, or of a local who done got out. A success. And I remember why I came.

"12? Shit I thought the economy was slow."

"It is. Why else you think there's 12 Mighty's?"

My cabbie has a Bills hat – new logo, not throwback – tilted at an angle, off to the side that throws constant glances of the charging Buffalo into the rearview, back over his shoulder, into my face. I take in the whirling, darkening decay of downtown around me, making my Milwaukee feel bustling, Chicago-esque almost. The 50 some bucks in my pocket feel multiplied into at least 100, the unemployment check that I'm quite certain will hit at midnight – about the time we'll pull into Mighty Taco's drive through – feel like one thousand. But what is money to me now? All I know is that we move through the darkness, past Seneca and Genesee, along a stinky river, and barrel up the deserted 190 toward an 80-some-year-old body that yearns for me; and that 3 beef-n'-cheese burritos will soon be procured, and that the cabbie, with that hat alone, has already ensured the reception of his week's biggest tip. And if I could tip everyone in town with a Bills hat… Upon me are the days of victory, the end times.

Every time I see my grandmother, she has grown smaller.

Shrunken, receded back away from life into her beleaguered skin. And the house around her is trying at the same. On a pleasant but aged blue-collar corner of Tonawanda, the house where my father was born and grew into a beer-swilling beast seems to shrivel around me. Maybe it's my own growing paunch, or the ego inflation from the miles and words covered since my visit of yesteryear, but it's certainly not what my grandmother says, what she always says upon first sighting her grandson in the doorway: "you've gotten so tall." "Grandma, I haven't grown an inch in 8 fucking years." "Oh the language!" And with that, we start. The burritos dangling from a plastic bag in my hand as her papery, droopy arms drape around me with all their might, grasping, full of relief and content and not wanting to let go, and I just got here. Maybe you can go home again. And the tears, oh they start, they try, but I've gotten too good, too-honed are the defense mechanisms, and I savor it, breath deep, grace the moment: "you're so excited to see me, you could at least put in your fucking *teeth*."

For the next 4 days, I bide my time, dreamily anticipate New York City growing in the windshield. Rest. Stretch my gut. Rest some more. Assume the position: semi-horizontal on the perfectly-stuffed Lazyboy-like rip-off, remote on arm rest, pillow propping my melon just enough to gaze at the outdated Sony dancing with "whatever you want to watch," as she says, repeatedly. And I let Grandma run her course, handle her like a river, with the respect you have to show when there clearly is no shutting it off, only managing it, keeping cool, and trying not to drown in the effusive offerings of brownies, tea, pie, candy, popcorn, eggs, brownies, tea, wine, ice cream sandwiches. The bombardment is near ceaseless, continuing even before we've finished our pizza, halting momentarily while we debate between 'The Sting' and 'The Apartment,' and then resuming into the evening.

"You're not going out, right?"

Longingly, full of hope, protection, with just a twist of looming disapproval once the credits roll and nothing is on but "Cheers."

"No grandma."

Through gritted teeth, no intonation, at this point of the day my frustration so over-cooked that I can no longer temper it with any kind of loving snark. I wish to, but all I can muster is a continued stare at the TV, silence, as she totters down the hall toward the bathroom, the old person shuffle of creeping arthritis at the end of a long day, her nightgown swaying side to side. And me, stuffed, ungrateful, no "I love you"'s or "Hope you make it through the night"'s, silent, vacantly flipping channels.

But go out, I do, carefully, easing the screen door shut behind me just after midnight. Feeling guilty about lying, about being dickheaded, about losing my cool with the nature's river, about the fact that I probably won't finish the pan of brownies she made specifically for my visit. So I walk and smoke over the sad streets, with their humble houses and cars in the driveway and TV lights flickering in dark living rooms behind closed shades. To the bar at the corner, toward my Labatts and Molsons and fried tips of heaven slathered in syrupy hot sauce which I then drown in bleu cheese; toward the Bills decked-out everyday folk, straight out of a Springsteen song, whom I can picture, easily, drinking with my dad; toward the wood-paneled confines of low expectations and homely contentedness, easy friendliness and facial hair and beer pooches and ZZ Top and then Dire Straits (oh! Shit! "Money for Nothing"!) blaring on the jukebox and the aww shucks yeah I'llhaveanotha Jim; toward what I left behind when my father died and my ma' remarried a man who could afford garbage disposals and tuition for fat dreamy sons, and thus moved the clan halfway across the country. And I fawn envy over the simplicity, noting the seeming absence in these parts, in this bar, of the midnight disease – that affliction that rattles my soul, shivers my eyelids as the rest of the world sleeps, that leads me out toward sky-gazing solitary smokes and corner bars in different cities.

Toward a lot, I walk, but more so, away, from what I know I will return to: The den, next to where my grandmother lay, snoring in her nightie under the grandpa-mounted wall crucifix. I will play the remembrance game, like any decent half-drunk, like I do with my high school yearbooks. The grandiose sentimentalities rushing over me, in waves – and I do the two-step waltz with the dusty shoeboxes from upper back-closet shelves. But there's something else, specific, painful here that the bar both helps put off, and prepares me for. It's a particular yellowed newspaper article, which has wriggled itself all the way from the Midwest into my grandmother's collection. Between frayed polaroids of my father, and my father's father, pics of Uncle John sporting full mustache by a Harley in front of this very house, others of various old folks looking universally younger and vastly 1970's-ish, between setlists of my brother's high school band, is a crinkly, tissue-thin newspaper document of my glorious reign on the tennis court. When, indeed, I was the Andre Agassi of my own little world.

Back then, when my face was caught squarely between the breadths of acne and the beginner's scraggly beard. When I was undeterred, unfettered, utterly unbothered by any trips to the airport, due to my impending, overwhelmingly imminent importance to the world. Existing still as a virgin, but so adept in the realms of 'everything but', so assured in knocking that wall down with the next foul swoop was I, that it didn't even matter. When wisdom-found was accompanied by the ginger steps of fresh rubber scented Nikes and not late night breaths of whiskey. Paradise coming in the back seat of a borrowed car, and not in the smoky, loud recesses of a dive. When a good Friday night was pizza rolls and ping-pong. When: "Teddy and Ry: A Fun Tandem To Watch" was an actual declaration inspired on the pen of some beautifully perceptive, bottom-feeder local sportswriter.

And a fun tandem we were. Me with my steady, unrazable grace, flowing and volleying, and Ry with his booming backhand returns, snarling fist pumps, and ravenous exultations of "Come ON!" after big points. Me, with an unerring crispness, the tactics covered "soundly" as the sportswriter decreed. He, almost always ready to punch a tough opponent, with a pulsing coiled energy, a vibration almost, his grip on the racket causing the inner forearm veins to bulge menacingly, always on the verge of *losing* it. As he did one night, apparently, one year ago, drunkenly flipping his beloved Jeep in the wee of the night over some twisty California roads, then deciding there was only one way to make the situation right. Or maybe there was no way to make the situation right – other than with a frenzied, spasmatic close dance with a green rope in the air out on the back deck of his Santa Barbara home. Or maybe he was, defiantly, done with rightness and situations and such. Either way, I picture him with an *at'll show 'em* fist pump, somehow, as if he just hit an ill-advised shot far too hard and it grazes the line for a winner, anyhow. I see him with an insolent sneer, a smirk almost. A *Gotcha!* to the opposing doubles team, to the whole world. I know it didn't happen this way, but maybe it did.

So there it sits before me. The paper growing faded and yellower all the time, every day, as my life, post-tennis, continues, sort-of, half-a-country away. The room's light probably the last still burning in the Tonawanda night, the city so defeated, blighted, consoling itself in warm beds. And my father and dead doubles partner laid out in paper on the carpeted den floor before me, as I sit Indian-style and try to stifle unmanly sobs. But they've come, blabberingly, sloppily with the scent of beer on my breathe, and of course I can already hear Grandma's slippered, worried shuffle down the hall, and I halt her as best as possible. "Go back to bed Grandma, sorry 'bout the noise, I was just, uh, Masterbating!" "Oh! Teddy!"...

And she turns and I can hear her close the door with a huff. And a Fuck You comes to my lips, softly, and then forcefully, and then Fuck You, near shouting, and I can only wonder what goes through Grandma's head as she can probably hear me, thinking me berating my body with candle wax, but one more comes anyway, and Fuck You. And now my only living grandmother thinks me a masochistic serial self-defiler, which will no doubt necessitate countless rosaries and cost her years of her life. So fuck you for that too. And I say it. And we used to be a fun tandem to watch and now I'm a sad sack on the floor, who's smoked more cigarettes in the past hour than times on the tennis court in the last year. A sad sack left to cover the whole court, myself. And fuck you because I can't hit those backhands, with that fearlessness on big points and seeming non-acknowledgement of the moment, of mortality. All by myself, with those big alleys. So, fuck you. And now I have to see your mom, with the caked makeup and drugged faraway look in her eyes like at the cemetery, and take our trips, alone, to San Francisco, getting stuck next to some Navy prick on the plane with little to no appreciation for the hops of Anchor Steam. And I have to chase your elusive 'nawlins voodoo tail. And I don't even remember what she looked like or what it was you said to make her smile that night with the beer and now that stuff, the only you and I stuff, you took it all with you. And I have to write the novel that won't go anywhere. And sing the blues. And have everybody ask what happened what happened what happened. So, fuck you. And the curses roll, with the tears and my grandma fingering the plastic rosary beads, probably, in her little widow bedroom, and a town in the muck dreams woozy 4am bar time dreams. While it's far too late for 'fuck you's, because the dirt is sticking and the worms do their worm work and the newspaper continues to yellow, even now, before my eyes.

Over breakfast – that lovingly-processed Velveeta so generously gooped, liquefied amidst the scrambled fluffs of eggs, with gleaming black-edged bacon, Land o' Lakes-doused rye toast, steaming, creamed Cream of Wheat, the hearty type of first-meal meant for fortifying before Buffalo winter days, or farming, or WWII or something - the game of catch-up continues.

Grandma: "Still with the writing?"

Me: "I got some things together."

And the coffee: not good, what old people drink, stale and burny, and all for the comfort and warmth and gullet-moistening, rather than the nuance, whiffs of grapefruit, passion fruit, whatever, that my palate has sophisticated toward.

"That why your going to New York?"

With her mouth full of toast crust, almost as if she didn't really want to ask, to hear the answer, to hear me lie somehow, but thinks she should. As if she can avert a fully-fabricated response by only half-mumbling the query.

"Yeah. Publishers." And my gaze is lost in the cheesy goop before me, delicious and sticky, clogging to itself and the plate as it must be, currently, to my lower intestine.

"Oh?"

"Yeah. Got some pieces too. *Think* pieces."

"Still dating Heather?"

"Her name *was* Amanda."

"And still with the trumpet?"

"Guitar Grandma, Guitar." Me, finding the old patience challenged a bit earlier in the day than normal...

"Well excuse me for living."

"Fine. Excused."

"Any prospects?" Again, with a sideways disinterested delivery through gulps of her third cup of coffee, each sip with an over-exaggerated sucking slurp, exclamation-pointed with a drawn out 'ahh…'

"They want me back at work."

"Oh, of course they do."

"Well, ya know, they let me go…"

"Oh, of course they want *you* back."

"But, you see, they *let* me *go*…"

"Are you happy there?" Her, like my mother, like my brother, like the consensus of the eyes all affix on me on the bus, fully accepting of the fact that I'm going back, that there really is no alternative, that I belong in some office, pushing papers, slinging boxes, getting behind the mule, that I don't have the words together, fully, or if I do, they are benign, a mere side vegetable to my prixe fixe future. And my gig on the splinter-top bench isn't going to get me booked on the road. And all those loving, dreamful hours. Spent for what? I might as well have been sleeping for the past seven months.

"Well, you know what I'd really like to do?"

"Not again with the taco fantasy!?" Her, incredulous, almost with a coffee spit-take, a grin, an accepting disbelief like every time when I inform her that the first thing I will do upon laying my travel boots on Buffalo dirt will be to render tacos.

"It's about more than the tacos, grandma."

"All you want to do is eat tacos."

And it's funny, how, with her, like maybe a stranger in a coma, like maybe a silently crazy man at my bus stop, something trustworthy lays in this lack of practical reception. So, like Costanza, just desperate to get the code of his chest, I go ahead – again – with my strange passion for a diminutive mariachi guitar player at my favorite taqueria. With my hopes to kidnap him, tie him in a burlap coffee sack, throw him in a windowless van, to bring him to my apartment, and set him up with a little blanket and pillow on the short living room love seat. The one by the window with the morning light. How happy we'd be. Oh, he'd get over the abduction thing, surely. Then it'd be just the two of us, him strumming softly when I awake, singing sweet and gentle as I pick my eye crust, taking away the morning's inherent sluggish pain, easing the passage of a pre-work dump from the other side of the bathroom door. And then when I get home, he's warmed, and plays more forcefully, with that crazy Mexican middle-finger strumming technique. And it's nothing to him. The ease with which his 5'2 frame handles the nylon strings, pausing between songs to sip a cerveza, or maybe tequila – the bottle of Don Julio I surprise him with one day from the liquor store, his eyes brightening. And we're together, with our guitars and pots and pans, and our little chorizo tacos and homemade morita salsa shared at the kitchen counter, him teaching me Spanish, me paying the heat bills. Hearty laughs. A jovial pat on the back for my constant mispronounciation of *mierda*. "No, no, *mee-el-dah* ahhaha." And then him back to la guitarra, at his spot on the couch, while I hum along at the sink and cleanse his taco grease driblets from the plates...

And so I've divulged my dreams, and this is the part where she might look in my eyes, and I'd find our family's entire lineage behind hers, right next to my purpose. And then Peter Gabriel's "Solsbury Hill" would start up somehow, loudly, and her heart would swell with pride, over something, and suddenly it's the next scene and everything is glimpsed from a far shot, and there I am, driving a car, windows down, smiling, radio blaring, toward something, toward digging something up, toward a thing from the past and maybe that old colonial on the other side of town. Where my father's ghost lurks. And I'd peruse his old beer can hiding places in the back yard, and ponder the dead patches of grass, and under a tree he planted when I was nothing more than a tailed spec swimming in his sac, there I might find my secret hidden strength, direction, something. Under the plaid I'd feel suddenly sprouted bushy hairs, my arms taking the shape of Uncle John's. At that moment I could even drive a stick shift. Suddenly, in cinematic denouement, there I am: A man of purpose, roots, wide shoulders, hairy forearms. Having figured it out, just like that, epiphany and revelation with the confession and the heart laid bare on the kitchen table next to the box of Tim Horton's crawlers.

But, instead, we're still there, and she's offering me post-meal strawberries, and I'm suppressing a fart, and all I hear coming to my lips, distantly, softly, is "I guess all I want is to never set my alarm clock."

And she gets it, with loving reproach, with a shake of the head: "Oh, that's all you've ever wanted."

Later, everything she says somehow comes back to the weather. Even when we both know we'll do nothing but stuff our faces and put off for a few hours our shared bottle of evening Merlot. Even though the only weather reports I currently care about are for a big city that isn't neglected by the Weather Channel's US map.

"We could go to the Falls."

"Ehhh."

"We could try the new fish fry place."

"Umm."

And maybe it's time to go when the breakfasts have become log-like in digestion, and my second cup of bad coffee needs to be taken on the toilet, and the drive through girl at Mighty Taco has suddenly come to know me solely by the sound of my voice, disembodied as it is hanging out the window of Grandma's Malibu. When the Lazy Boy knockoff feels lumpy beneath my distended, sweatpants-ed gut, or is that actually my colon?

And then, by day 4, there is this: "It'd be a nice day for the cemetery."

"There really are no nice days for the cemetery."

"Oh, you don't care about seeing your grandfather, your *Father*?"

And this is leveled with such head-shaking acceptance at my heartlessness, and I immediately flash on Uncle John all those 3,000 miles away, and know, in one sum, why men need, crave California. It's time to leave, and she seems almost to have shrunken just since I arrived. Barely 4'5 if I had to guess, and what, again, is the cutoff of dwarfdom? And I half-joke to myself that next time, I'll have to watch that I don't step on her.

"You're getting tall, you know that?" Her, still, with the insistence.

"Not an inch in 8 goddamn years. You're fucking shrinking."

"Oh, the language…"

But there's little deflective wit left by the time she releases me from a hug, and I pull away in a cab and watch her fade back into the house's emptiness, offering a meek wave, her hand barely at tit-level, as if that's as high as she can go, as much as she can stand to wish me adieu, her little body molding together with the screen door in my eyes as the distance grows, and she shrinks. I feel my heart opening outward to the fading Tonawanda streets, thinking, as I do every time, I'll call her every day. My cabbie is sporting a Bills hat – throwback logo– and he envies my big-dicked voyage to the big-dicked City. But he loves his town, even his Sheridan Avenue, and his waterfront as we glimpse it to the right, heading south and downtown. "So great, to get over here, see the river." And it's so sad, putrid and void of all beauty, raped by the highway and I can't tell if he's being ironic. I almost laugh, for a hazy stench seems to be rising from the blighted waterway, somehow growing stronger, even as we speak. There's a sailboat out there, ok, yes, and the hulking bridges, and maybe some rugged steel belt charm, but to tell it – currently, too much for the bloated sack in the backseat. By now spent, void of emotion, so possessed with the urge to flea it feels I could only have, indeed, *come* from Buffalo. "Solsbury Hill" doesn't play. Instead it is local talk radio and the yaps yapping on the dawning Bills season. 'If''s fill the air. 'Maybe''s. Wonder, but, not really. Resignation. A tinge of bitterness.

"How you liking the Bills this year?"

"Arrgh," is all he can muster from the back of his throat, shrugging, lifting his hat by the brim and scratching his scalp before pulling it back down.

And we drive on, and I think that maybe I could live here. And I think I could also gulp the littered Niagara River till it filled my lungs. But I probably won't do either. I'll go on, toward Amtrak, and smoke a cigarette on the platform, and wait for the man with the funny hat to come and take me down the line.

23

Not that a wreck, a derailment, an audible thump, face-covered bug-eyed screams, even a great lurch should be expected any time that an Amtrak train runs a man over. As mine just has. Certainly the big gruesome gray cars are built to absorb such force and carnage. Built to churn 'em up, carry on, protect the passengers and not let some suicidal sack or headphoned rail-jogger interfere with the important business of carrying on down the tracks. Obviously skin and bone are no comparison to the brute, chugging inertia of the machine: a 20-something-car conglomerate steel centipede. Barreling. Thrusting. Taking some miles – *miles!* – to come anywhere nears a complete stop. Offering, basically, the epitome of what man can tell steel to do. The imperialistic, forced malleability. But you'd at least expect something, when it inevitably happens, and the guts and whatnot are spewed and discharged and exploded all around the noble, unstoppable nose. *Something.* Not just to have your head down over some Frederick Exley, and be sipping bad coffee, and have the little light on and be near halfway between Albany and NYC, and feel the annoyance of an unexplained slowdown, and then an eventual, almost begrudging full stop, and then an approaching infringement on the big-city itinerary, and then a measly explanation of "trespasser activity," followed by ho-hums and guffaws from the seats and the people stretching in the aisles. All of them acting like it was a weather delay, a mechanical failure, some major nuisance on their forward-leaning lives. All: still in everyday-mode. Reflexively and logically processing, being pushed along the tracks, their minds half-observing and half-distracted in the green or blue or multi-colored collective glow of whatever wireless device was in hand. None of their temperaments trained for the inkling of something else entirely, maybe.

A bit later though, in the snack car, as I go for a too-many-dollars Heineken – prices which become seemingly reasonable by hour two and then downright bargain-like by hour 5 of the 400-mile trek – I see the telling interaction as I try to keep my train legs steady at the bar. One of the funny hats, stepping out from a sliding bathroom door, spotting a cohort, says to one of the other funny hats: "got that trespasser off the tracks, eh?" But it's in the smirk. Just like that, knowing I should have went to the bathroom first, skipped the beer break, anything that might have prevented my presence in this car at this exact moment. It is clear. That transcendent, knowing look of conspirators, all the desperate, preening humor of the gallows, contained in a simple co-worker-like glance. A look that's only deepened by the cold repetitions that like-employees must share. Must embark upon. The detached cynicism, obviously, is here so greatly needed, what with the whole operation of such mechanics of death, calamity, torso-exploding centripetal force. I can feel the chills begin their way down the spine, toward my butt. I feel something leave my stomach. Feel myself shiver. *Did anyone else see that?* Me, looking around. *Anybody feel a bump back then?* Wide-eyed, I turn toward the bartender, looking for assistance, maybe a laugh. Its a pseudo-bar at best, but about now some folksy wisdom, filtered through a hi-ball, might go toward easing the newfound shivering in my knees. He's merely annoyed though, clearing his throat, forcing a grin. Waiting for another dollar. I gave him a five. Only a five, and he sees it everyday. The high-velocity world of six-buck beers.

Again, there I am, big-city rough with his collar up to the wind (at least it would be up to the wind if those old-school little platforms between cars were still open for Hitchcockian homicide attempts and poetic, fast-moving smoke breaks) and Jack London's guide to hoboing tucked cozily into my spring jacket, sitting with a beer bottle warming between my thighs, hitting 'play' again, turn-

161

ing to gaze, watching the world darken, literally, out my windows. Yes, nice work, Ski. Your feet have been thrown. Now, officially, magnanimously and undoubtedly, murderously even, the force of that footprint has been waged, cemented, after all.

By the time we pull into Penn Station, unceremoniously, in the dark with no hint of that approaching skyline of utter immensity before us, through the back door it almost feels, the obvious nagging thought comes: I must look. Verify, know. Like a hit-and-run driver, driven to nip the haunting questions in the bud. Or one pondering if he needs to put it in reverse, hit the gas, and finish the deed. So I ignore the herds, exhaustedly shuffling, leading their luggage toward the stairs and their big-business, big-tourist plans, and mosey myself in the direction of the front of the train. Behind the conductor, stealthy. Picking a sweating train wedgie. Feeling drunk, obsessive-compulsive, Nancy Drew-like, my feet maintaining mischievous minds of their own. But a peek is all, some carnage to-go, and I'll be on the way.

But the city calls too. New York City: Just up those stairs and through the station – that overcooked crockpot of people and potential directions. The tug feels both ways. *I just wanna see his face...* Almost at the last second, halfways-up the front car, my sense of drama at a Marv Albert-fourth quarter pitch, my arm pits running accordingly, just before rounding the jet-like hulk of brutal, vengeful steel, stinking of grease and oil, looking guilty, plainly guilty and unremorseful, I turn. Many are caught returning to the scene of a crime. Not me – too smart. Not this time. Let the ghosts come as they may. *Think I got no ghosts?* Instead, I heed the call of the city above my head.

24

You've come this far, and still, with nothing to say.

Sitting in the East Village, in a French bistro on sunny St. Mark's Place, staring pensively into a sweating glass of Peroni, my brother – Colin, or 'Stalin', as he's aptly known – suddenly by my side, is chiding me for my incommunicative ways.

"You know me, I let my fists do the talking."

He's flown in, from southern Ohio, last minute-like. And while I had pictured, had always pictured, the final journey, the terminal jaunt, the dead man walking, that last-five-minutes-cab-to-the-airport scene – back-lighted by some Elliot Smith or some such maudlin strumming – being taken alone, all dramatic, forlorn and courageous, shoulders stiff and hardy against the wind, his all-at-once show-up seems appropriately Moriarty-esque. So lovingly intrusive, so overzealously chummy. Coming, graciously as it did, just minutes after I had implicated myself in the upstate hit n' run homicide, his voice, over the phone, pleading for inclusion – the same hope I used to read on his face after he had set a pick and begun to roll toward the basket in my pre-Ewing years on the hardwood – I had to let him have it. Be thankful for it. An accomplice. Again. "You need someone to show you around New York." And this too, I could let him have, even as I fingered the loose-structured itinerary jutting out of my tit-pocket. All those numbers, all those numbered streets.

Stalin: Me, plus 30 pounds and 5 years, fifty-percent less hair atop his melon, and a cache of razor-sharp, Benson-quick guitar licks. Occasionally, during a long run, on his Gibson, primarily, E-dash-something or other, he unleashes this pinkie finger pull-off technique that I have difficulty discussing: as if his fretting hand's fifth finger has the length of his index, has the ability to pull back within itself, then instantly jump out, span the gap of two, three frets, and continue thusly in tight rhythmic propulsion over multiple bars – like it was the tongue of a lizard, snapping at notes for sustenance, then retracting to procure flavor. In somehow perfect time – even in front of other people, ears, eyes.

Together, we've eschewed a near-perfect near-fall day, unanimously decided against its merits, and the outdoor seating, with no discussion, and have tucked ourselves in the back corner, the only two save for the tender, our elbows resting on the bar.

"You have to get over something, Teddy." Him, as I take a deep sip, feel the wonder of mid-day, early-vacation hops down my throat.

"It's a bit early in the day for that talk." Now his turn to gulp, and to placate the post-flight giddiness.

"No, not that."

"…"

"It's that you have a bit of an aversion, to reality."

"Fuck you."

And to that, we both drink.

We have wandered down a certain path, one I thought we'd not tread, at least until the beers turned to the 3am variety, the kind such gravity generally necessitates. Or, the kind that necessitate such gravity. It's often hard to take him seriously – he of the nature of 'the artist,' breathing to create, working, barely, merely to keep strings on the shiny vintage guitars and sustenance in his considerable gut, fuel for more gigs, more late-night blow sessions. Now though, he seems, almost, maybe, genuinely concerned. For a moment this alarms me.

"You fly back Sunday?" Him, verifying the most negligible aspect of the trip.

"Correct."

"And, you're supposed to have work – when? – Monday?"

"That's debatable."

"Well, you should know, I have orders, direct from the top, not to leave you until you call your boss, confirm you're coming in Monday."

"You probably also have orders from mom to keep me out of Harlem."

"Well, actually, yeah…"

A grin collectively punctures each one of our four over-fed cheeks.

"And you know we's going to Harlem."

Never before had I known it, but the best way to experience the island is while awaiting the coming glow, the inevitable weekly charity, that most deserved influx of Uncle Sam bread. My darling unemployment check. Like a new friend at a bar, the conversation coming so natural, almost too easy, with one topic bleeding into the next, one commonality giving way to another mutuality, sports going to music going to food going to sports as music metaphor to *what are ya gonna eat later?*, laughs seguing to high fives and beers bought for one another, I begin to wonder - will it be weird to ask for his number? Should I try to keep in touch? I fall in love too easy. And can already feel myself missing the bank account penetrations. Growing nostalgia over the warm and fuzzies shared. Unsure, I'm still hopeful that the feeling is reciprocal: *ohh, remember that Friday night back in 'nawlins? Man, we had a time… How about when I almost took the bus – and then I remembered you, and was all, 'Nope'! And got a cab?* And we laugh. Arm-in-arm almost, me and this invisible, benevolent hand, skipping through the rain.

Here though, I'm averting a reality near as nice. Together, freshened from our Gramercy Park temporary-digs, coffees in hand, just-emerged out of the 96th street subway station – Stalin, navigating a tricky transfer around mid-town, me, close in tow, reverting to little-bro passenger mode for the first time in years, it feeling right, decent – we have but a sliver of Central Park to make our own before we round the corner, and head across the street - 110th. Immediately, the song begins - cheesy strings, synths, loose-wrist, rapid-fire right hand rhythm guitar action – in my head, on our lips, trading lines, half-humming, half-mumbling substitutes for the unknown words, just dying to get back to the refrain. Which we hit the second time as soon as our feet land on the dark, mysterious promised land – 'Across.' Bobby Womack pay dirt. And we turn left, toward chicken and waffles, and my phone is out, ready to check the account. I find it already ringing though, the blinking 'incoming' informing me that my mother would like to talk, nag, cajole.

"Can't talk now, mom, lost in Harlem." It comes too easy.

"Ohh! Well, I told him!…"

"Just kidding, but really, I don't get no reception up here, it's like a jungle, have to call you back."

Like that, something is dealt with, my brother with a sudden shit-eating grin that I recognize from somewhere, near bursting with amusement, now lighting two Camels in his mouth, handing me one as I dial my bank's toll-free number. Holding his breathe, all four of our pits by now streaming with the apprehension, the day's unseasonable heat, and the subway's lingering swampiness. And like we know – with the Harlem at hand, and the hunger, and the swallowing New York City-ness, there being no question as to the merits of the gods – the check has hit. And hit hard. The sun, sensing dawning importance, like in such a book where a writer bothers and bothers and trips and tumbles to describe the pillows of clouds and all that bullshit business, it seems to emerge at this moment. The song continues, with an added lilt in our voice, a jolt in our hungover steps. Not only fried chicken ahead, not only syrup-slobbed fried-sponge-like goodness, but, now, sides of mac n' cheese, too. This will be our lot.

Past the storefronts, and Puerto Rican-looking dudes unloading crates of fruit, little neighborhood kids with their rambunction, brick apartment buildings lining the illustrious borderline, the northern vestiges of the park, over there, just back across 110th street. And we can't stop with the singing; though, we know, aside from the refrain, absolutely none of the lyrics.

The jazz n' samba, the jazz n' samba, everything swinging, and the pizza joints and the cabs bursting down 6th Avenue, and up, too, and the zig-zagging and angled and semi-circled Village streets, like lunatic cousins to the rigid grids of Manhattan maps, even one named for Dave Van Ronk over there, 4th avenue intersecting 4th street – what? And with the lights and everything going, swirling, teeming, and just down a few steps, with a duck of the head, a nod to the bouncer, smiling and happy to see me in my clever side whiskers and knowing cap, our feet and elbows and ears have found home on Christopher Street.

We joke about the Stonewall Inn next door, we jive about guitars, we snigger at mom, we clasp backs and then fold our arms across chest and then talk emphatic-like with our hands and figure shit out and get 'notherone's, and it all happens with beat, energy, pinache or some fucking French word. Us in love, buzzing with the surroundings, pulsing, trying to keep cool, keeping mostly cool, maybe, as we order Brooklyn Lagers.

Our one true concern at the moment though, is to find out how we can not relinquish our spots at the dark mahogany bar, and still manage to get high before the jazz guitar "god" (Stalin's words), that Uncle Sam has covered the cover for, takes the stage. Or the corner, really, that substitutes for a stage. We decide, in the hushed tones of public potheads everywhere, on the one-at-a-time-go-outside method. Each of us, smitten with our lofty logic, takes his turn with the fake-cig one-hitter contraption. Just out the door and around the corner, and then back. And nobody noticing, because we're bad. And now the air is carrying our little floral plumes up toward the peaks, the Rockefellers and the Chryslers, and over the river toward Jersey, and couples go hustling by, in their big-city pace, focusing on the serious business of Saturday night fun-getting in their complicated shoes. Places. Plans. Eight million flutters for something to matter on this night. And I hurry back in for the hand-off, back to sit down, toward my seat and little domicile amidst the madness.

And maybe the crowd is half Asian tourists, and maybe not, it doesn't really matter, such is that thing here – that most clichéd and over-abused term: *vibe*. It floats around, through the Christmas lights, draped non-chalantly, through Mike Stern's bent notes. Together with bass and drums backing, he straddles genres, smiles, bounds up and down the neck. The groove is palpable, the full bar silent in respectful anticipation, the only non-music noise the placement of drinks atop the bar or tables, the tender quiet and efficient, working with points and nods as much as possible, glancing at me and silently mouthing 'a nother', me with a thankful nod in reply, the gentle *'ting'* of the old-school cash register accentuating beats. Folks hurry by the windows at street level – some heading east, toward the East Village, some heading west, toward the West Village. And me, settled, between, at ease here.

My hazy mind is clear with revelation and contentedness. This is where a guy could get down to his serious business, could quench that dusty old desire, that romantic tug, the favorite utterance and the reason to attempt said verb: 'to write.' Basically, before me, how I want to live: surrounded by the possibility of books, screenplays, works of art, compositions, the hint, the whisper, soundtracked by relentless bop and such, the energy resounding and bouncing off the bar and beer taps and wood-paneling and framed Dexter Gordon pics. The possibility of poetry, languid, hanging, in the ether right around, before me. But the actual act, the actual business of it all more comprised of drinking beers, sitting.

Sitting, as we are now, one scotch and two half-finished pint glasses before us, the place clearing out around, the band packing up in the corner. It's sometime after 2, and they're joshing with the bartender, a couple stray half-drunk Asian girls half-flirt the big-grinned guitarist. A man just-off work. Satisfied, pleased with a day's labors. And now we've garnered a prime spot, in the corner by the window, sipping. Fogging consciousness, leaning toward answers and other-city drunkenness, also known as early-adult euphoria.

But Stalin, or 'ol' bro' as I've begun referring to him at by now, him assuming a status of esteem and prominence after his 4th Johnnie Black – feels ready to go, for more, to maintain the Moriarty role. I feel his pull out the door, and, fuck it, think, maybe it's good.

"C'mon anywhere you want to go." He's amped, crazy-eyed, already non-clandestinely, flauntingly plugging up the one-hitter on the street.

"Well, the itinerary says at the Fat Cat…"

"Fuck the itinerary."

"Feel like I've heard that before."

"C'mon, less' getta cab, anywhere, I'm paying."

"…"

And I flash on Uncle John, lighting a Marlboro as we stand on this other coast; and Bean, in the middle, probably turning his big car down a forgotten slice of old Chicago, fresh bowl or Taco Bell on my seat; and Ewing, rounding my parents' street, maintaining that mercantile relationship agreement whereby he brings them their dinner and mom eats great pizza and pretends she doesn't think her two sons are about to get knived and raped and possibly raped with a knife in a Harlem alley, and tips Ewing so that he can buy cheap beer and drink it in the 'zebo and gaze at the pond and 'member when with tears and smiles; and Hill, with his finger under his nose, pondering big legalese type words, counting his suits; and the boss, probably in plaid pants on a golf course, like all bosses, and wondering why I haven't called, checking his phone with furrowed brow while doing that dickhead leg-over-leg and lean on the driver stance that golfers do; and the guitar player, thumping and humping for underserving tourists in the Quarter still; and my cockroach friend, dead still, on his back still, in that pissy outdoor bathroom that never gets cleaned; and my Severance, the rich friend I never deserved, never loved enough; and all the gaggle of cats I know, with the all-day sleeping and endless anus licking; and the Hell's Angels and their every which way pounding; and the Navy dude and his pants with the starch; and the Roomate with the job and the car and the ties; and every cab driver that will never, could never know me; and every bartender at the end of every night who wanted to go home – *just, please, can you let me go home?* – who never shooed this thirsty fuck with the questions; and Marv Albert noticing, observing, dramatizing us all in our little games; and Grandma, alone, for some reason still at the window, in my mind, waving goodbye. And somewhere a distant Illinois graveyard grows colder with the night air. And Ry's parents wait for the pain to subside, for the breaths to come normal again, for something to laugh at, for it all to be over, sitting in the living room and looking at their big front door that holds back, but doesn't, a world that treated them to the worst it has. A door that I should knock, but won't.

"Ya know what?" Me, emboldened, a bit, balling a fist, surging, realizing there are two kinds of people in the world – the something, something, whatever kind, and the kind that drive mad and drunk and aimless toward the middle of Manhattan. And I say it:

"Fuck the itinerary."

"Yesss. Where do you wanna go? Anywhere in the city." Ol' bro, with a Larry Bird fist pump, jolly, rocking back and forth on each foot, eyes expectant.

"The Bronx."

"How 'bout Times Square?"

"Only if you get in the cab, and declare 'Times Square and Step on It.'"

"Done."

And he does, unabashedly, frightening, almost, to the Pakistani who turns the yellow race car right on 6th Avenue and burns north, uptown, weaving in and out and straddling lane lines like they were mere suggestions. Ignoring blasts of horns while simultaneously laying on his own, jibbering into his blue tooth in a distant tongue, with two Skis in the backseat, gazing, wide-eyed, out and up.

"New York is best seen from the back seat of a speeding taxi."

"Who said that?"

"I did, just now."

And we laugh.

Whirling, with alacrity and velocity through the buildings as they gain height and the street signs grow bolder and higher in number. My brother, now suddenly punching my arm with excitement, feeling especially elevated. Maybe because he came, maybe because of the Scotch, possibly because he plays better than what we've just seen, and *knows it*. Owns it, really. His bald head will rest easy on the cushy hotel pillow tonight, satisfied in the boozy, but accurate, notions of comradeship. Existence on the level. My jealousy is tinged with pride, and vice versa and all that. Of course I have something of my own too, *ya know?* It's a walloping 50 pages of only-slightly awkward poetic prose. Antiquated, maybe. Kerouac-copping, sure. But oh, the dark irony. The clever turns of phrase!

171

The bleeding heart insight! Fifty pages - if I double space. *But the tenderness!*

And the stories and the clichés of this big giant of a city wash over my head, as I put down the window and breathe deep, and think about expanding my book, my work, my efforts, and making an imprint on this New York. How I might Force myself upon it, maybe like a rapist, though I've never been much good at metaphors. As we barrel toward mid-town and my brother forces his will, his money, his jazz, his highly-developed fretting technique, his enthusiasm, all over me. And I take it, standing up – figuratively – and smiling, I savor it, swallow it whole, ask for more with hungry eyes, drunkenly daydream myself over a typewriter, capturing it all in courageous all-night bouts. My fault and my way are linked, and a change in course now feels, rightly, impossible. Especially now, what with the cab's deranged speed and all. The driver is obviously hungry to dump us, already scanning for the next fare, and we're somewhere in the 50's, and the hugeness is opening up, and I lean forward toward the next drink, the next stop, a brief respite before another go-round. Seeing my own smirk now on my brother's face, I picture us from afar, together but a blip in the teeming, blinding 3am madness. I turn toward him, and seemingly with all unbridled might, ball my fist, and punch his arm.

Epilogue

Afternoon is breaking, and my brother has left me to my own devices. Which is his first mistake. Off to spend his last day and night with some musician buddies in Brooklyn – another fraternity, brotherhood, another for me to feel apart of. And he has trusted me – mistake two – to raise my booze-soaked and beleaguered body from the mattress and go forth. *To earn, to contribute…* Here, it's easy to spot the failure in logic, arising as it did, from one distinct moment of eye contact the previous night: Mike Stern picking up his Telecaster, ready for work to begin, me, back at the bar, turning, looking out the door, frantically trying to assure he not miss the start of the show, and spotting him. Outside, cigarette smoke was billowing, framing his face, which held a stony, fat-cheek grin. Seeing me, nodding slightly, understanding, plopping the butt back into his mouth, sucking with last-drag finality between thumb and forefinger, he flicked the half-spent Camel at the street and began moving back inside, toward the bar, casually, unhurriedly, convincing. An agreement was waged between our locked eyes: all is well.

But now its two hours until my flight, 15 minutes till check-out, and the bed is soft and the AC unit humming. I have no inkling as to the plan to arrive my person at the airport. All I know is that it is boroughs – *boroughs!* – away. And the mere term fatigues me further. And the cell phone alarm is ringing – the signal to get up, put feet on the ground, wash the zit cream from my face, pack my dirty boxers, take some aspirin, maybe brush my teeth, become presentable. Move. But instead, I'm hitting 'snooze.' Another 10 minutes won't make or break this life. And I'm burrowing back in, and then, time lapsing, I'm hitting 'snooze' again, and then the alarm won't stop, interfering with floating wisps of senseless dreams, infuriating me, really. To the point, where in a moment of weird solo demonstrativeness, I lower the covers, reach and pull back the blinds from bed, and shake my fist. Through the chilled air, at the life flow of East 17th street below me, at the throbbing hangover, at the son-of-a-bitch sun. And now – what? 10?, 20? - minutes past checkout time, it won't be long before they start with the banging on the door, ready my credit card number for further ruthless extraction. And 'fuck it' I say, turning over and establishing an especially comfortable position, on my side, spooning my secondary pillow. Turning back over 10 minutes later, to hit 'snooze'. Now putting the pillow over my face. Now hitting 'snooze' again. The next time not even checking the time. And then again. And now with two pillows over my head, the precise spot of the cell phone on the nightstand known through muscle memory, not even needing to look, to raise my head. And hitting it again, and the sun shining through the blind cracks, and fuck it, and I hit 'snooze.'